RIDE THE WILD COUNTRY

RIDE THE WILD COUNTRY

by

Chap O'Keefe

Dales Large Print Books
Long Preston, North Yorkshire,
BD23 4ND, England.

British Library Cataloguing in Publication Data.

O'Keefe, Chap
Ride the wild country.

A catalogue record of this book is
available from the British Library

ISBN   1-84262-461-X pbk
ISBN   978-1-84262-461-6 pbk

First published in Great Britain 2005 by Robert Hale Limited

Cover illustration © Prieto by arrangement with
Norma Editorial

Published in Large Print 2006 by arrangement with
Robert Hale Ltd.

Dales Large Print is an imprint of Library Magna Books Ltd.

Printed and bound in Great Britain by
T.J. (International) Ltd., Cornwall, PL28 8RW

For
JIM GRIFFIN
of the State of Connecticut
Volunteer Horse Patrol,
equine expert and Texas Rangers *fan,*
in appreciation of helpful advice

1

FIGHT IN FRISCO

In the hazardous life of Joshua Dillard a sudden departure was no extraordinary occurrence. And a gunfight was often the indicator that it was time for him to vamoose, light out, ride on. Disappear.

Regardless of the inherent rights and wrongs of the particular situation, staying around after a shooting affray could be unhealthy. Along would come not only the vengeful associates of the deserving recipients of Joshua's lead, but also reputation-hungry kids eager to prove themselves quicker on the draw, more accurate in placing a killing shot; the ones who lusted to inherit his unwanted gunfighter mantle.

Thus it befell that Dillard was obliged to quit San Francisco one late summer morning several days before his scheduled departure.

Though he'd been down on his luck, things had been looking brighter. Confident of having an assignment lined up which promised to replenish his severely depleted purse (a not-unusual circumstance), Joshua had been determined to enjoy his last few days in the city.

Safely putting aside his railroad fare for Greeley, Colorado, via Cheyenne, Wyoming, he'd carefully counted out the last coins and bills in his poke and set forth to sample the pleasures of a metropolis regarded by its eulogists as America's Paris on the Pacific – rich, cosmopolitan, cultured, sophisticated.

He walked the streets of the city and saw sideshows of gymnastic monkeys and howling dervishes, fortune-tellers and patent medicine dealers. Oriental carpets and Chinese brocades lent alien colour to shop windows.

Joshua hadn't seen fit to afford accommodation at hotelier William C. Ralston's showy new Palace, built at a cost of $6 million. 'Seven-hundred-thirtysome rooms, every other with a private bath. A glass-roofed Palm Court, fountains and Doric columns, statues and all. Now that's what I call a hotel,' he'd lamented.

But he could therefore spare the *dinero* to go calling at an august Frisco parlour house, said to cater for the more discerning gentleman. Long a widower and not addicted to casual dalliance, Joshua Dillard was none-theless a red-blooded male. He took a hack from Market Street to the Russian Hill section, just north of Nob Hill where the high-society folks lived.

On a street with commanding views of the bay, Joshua glimpsed flags of many nations flying from the masts of ships tied up alongside the wooden wharves and jetties. The hack driver dropped him off outside an imposing, three-storey red-brick mansion surrounded by a low wall and pillars of the same brick supporting wrought-iron railings painted a glossy black. A red lantern hung discreetly in the front porch.

Elegant, civilized, Joshua thought.

To his mild disappointment, the decor inside the house was a little too sumptuous, too lavish for the nicest of taste. Shiny varnish had been applied to all panelling and doors, probably rubbed down with pumice between the several coats to give a mirror finish. The upholstered furniture was over-stuffed and the walls throughout covered with a flock paper. The paper's large repeating pattern, deep-pink fleurs-de-lis, would have put a client a few decades later in mind of cotton candy.

Looking-glasses, of which there were disconcertingly many, were framed with ornate, gold-leafed scrollwork.

But the decadent surroundings didn't distract Joshua from taking his pleasure with 'Louise', a petite and willing blonde of eighteen, allegedly French but with a distinctly Irish accent. She employed the arts she'd learned and the delights nature had bestowed upon her with attentive enthusiasm. Joshua was rapt.

His thoughts were less favourable an hour or so later. 'Well, I'll be a sonofabitch!' he growled.

'Indeed it is ye'll be a frisky colleen's ruin,' the blonde, spread and spent, said, from the well-braced bed in the adjoining room. 'What would be the problem, boyo?'

'I've been cleaned out is the problem, sweetie. Robbed.'

Someone with fingers more nimble than Louise's had gone through the pockets of his clothing – discarded carelessly beside the still-steaming zinc tub of scented bath water where their transaction had begun with a tantalizing mutual lathering using a versatile bar of slippery pink soap.

The thieves had reduced his roll of greenbacks by half, craftily re-rolling the bills less tightly. They'd also taken some coin and other small, tradeable items, including a clasp-knife, though not his gunbelt and .45 Colt Peacemaker. The gun was well-worn and scarred by a crack in the blackened right grip.

Now the clasp-knife held considerable sentimental value. It had been a gift from his wife, who'd later been murdered in San Antonio, Texas. The day the Wilder gang had come calling, wrecking their home, snuffing out the warming flame of her beautiful young life, was the day that had put Joshua Dillard onto different trails forever.

He'd been possessed by an obsessive hatred of lawbreakers, which inclined him to recklessness. He'd resigned his position as an operative of the famous Allan Pinkerton Detective Agency. He'd become a free agent; a soldier of fortune. Ready to take chances; ready to kill those who offended his sharpened sense of justice.

When he saw that his wife's present had been taken by petty thieves, Joshua saw red. Too many things had been taken off him in this life. Big things, little things. Sometimes he had trouble in discriminating one from the other, but not this time.

Once dressed, he stormed down the

sweeping staircase to the parlour house's rococo ground-floor entrance hall and into the madam's office.

'Right, you old cow,' he said, flinging back the highly varnished oaken door with a crash. 'I want to know who sneaked into Louise's dressing-room and pilfered my belongings.'

At a guess, it wasn't the first time the woman had been faced with this situation, but Joshua's ferocity was of a singularly savage order.

A maturing, roly-poly woman, much done up in paint, red satin, Brussels lace and fake jewellery, she pulled herself to her feet.

Her gown's shiny fabric stretched and heaved over her bosom; her rouged cheeks quivered. 'Pilfered? Here?' she huffed. 'I never heard of such a thing!'

'You're a lying toad,' Joshua said.

Though clearly an intelligent woman in the operation of her successful business, and possibly an exciting and glamorous figure earlier in her professional life, she had the stamp of something besides the ravages of a past sensuality on her now.

Greed? Fear?

Off to his left, Joshua's keen eyes spotted the surreptitious movement of a beringed

14

hand, hidden from his direct view by the bulk of a mahogany desk, but revealed in one of the many mirrors that supposedly multiplied the establishment's visual delights. Distantly, he heard the muffled peal of a bell.

Consequently, when two men ghosted up behind him, one with gun in hand, he was ready for their intervention seconds before it was signalled in another of the tell-tale mirrors.

'How dare you, sir!' the madam was saying. 'I've never heard the likes of such a insult. Despicable. I'll have you know this is an orderly run house.'

But Joshua was turning from her and her shrill objection with the speed of a striking snake.

'Throw the bum out!' shrieked the madam. She didn't know how different he was from the pathetic suckers who were the normal run of her bawdy-house clients.

Joshua beat down the surprised first bouncer's gun arm, grabbed the wrist and twisted it. At the same time, he rode the man back into his companion, sending the pair of them crashing into the opened door.

The men were big fellows, real toughs of prizefighter build. The door buckled and slammed against the pink flock wall. The whole building seemed to shake. The drawn gun fell simultaneously from suddenly nerveless fingers. The safety was off and it discharged ear-splittingly in the close confines of the room.

The madam screamed. Elsewhere in the house, other females raised a wailing chorus like scared cats.

The second man recovered first. He lammed a punch at Joshua's mouth which split Joshua's lips and jerked his head back as though it was attached to a neck of rubber.

Joshua's wits were shaken for but a moment. Dropping under the following punch, he rammed the top of his head under the assailant's jaw and sunk his fists, one-two, into the fellow's belly, which put him out of the fight, gasping for breath, near-senseless.

The first tough dived toward his dropped gun. Joshua jumped on his back, smashing him face down on the carpet. He stomped a second and third time. Right foot, left foot. The prone man writhed in agony. 'Stop it, fer Chris'sakes,' he moaned. 'Yuh'll break m'back.' Mad with pain and the fear that he was permanently crippled, he, too, was done fighting.

Joshua's head carried on ringing – from

16

the blow he'd received in the face or from the women's screaming, he didn't know which. Yet luck was still with him.

For when a third man sneaked up on him, he wasn't taken by surprise, but again saw the threat coming like it was converging on him in several of the mirrors. This man had the mark of the other pair, but was older and somehow more intelligent and smarter-clothed and groomed. He was also hauling out a revolver, and his index finger was about the trigger, whitening, tightening. All this in not more than deathly split-seconds.

The whole thing was over in instants. Joshua drew his Colt with a speed the new-comer didn't know was possible. Tongues of flame spat from the muzzles of both guns. Two shots crashed out. A mirror exploded in a shivering cascade of glass shards. The room filled with the acrid reek of swirling gunsmoke.

And through it Joshua saw the blood spurting hideously from a punctured artery in his victim's neck like a grotesque red fountain as he toppled backwards, firing his gun a last time by some dying reflex of his trigger finger.

More screams rang through the house.

'You've killed Victor Porteous, you crazy

bastard!' the madam cried. 'Now you'll be for it. He's a big wheel in this city. They'll hang you for sure.'

A man of his rugged world, Joshua knew that most of the West's parlour house women were in debt to somebody. The girls were in debt to the madams who boarded them and clothed them in their finery. The madams were in debt to the vice lords who owned their properties and sometimes themselves. The dead man was this madam's principal no doubt, forced to take an active hand by his hired thugs' incompetence.

'Ain't no more than a dead Barbary Coast pimp in my book,' he said.

Then he blew the smoke from his Colt, holstered it and strode out.

A chill morning fog, with the barest hint of daybreak, found Joshua Dillard riding the Union Pacific Railroad out of the city. Ahead of the train lay the ascent of the Sierras and the suggestion in the east of a fierce sunshine and brilliant sky inland.

Safely aboard the passenger car, Joshua lifted the broad flat brim of the black hat that had partly concealed his hard, unshaven face during a hasty walk through the San Francisco streets to the railroad depot.

In fact, no one had paid him more than scant attention at that early hour. The sidewalks had been heaped with market produce – thousands of water melons and cantaloups, cucumbers and squashes, as well as crates of tomatoes, grapes, peaches, pears and apricots, all of enormous Californian size. He'd dodged between stack and pile while other early-risers had been taken up with earning their livelihoods.

From a pocket in his shabby black coat, he drew out his last letter from a Leigh Jordan in New York City. Jordan had unspecified business in the less-established reaches of the new state of Colorado. Dillard's name had been recommended by former Pinkerton comrades as a suitable companion for travels in a wild and rugged country where civilized settlement was sparse.

Dillard, it was said, didn't balk at the unorthodox. It was also implied that he wasn't beyond stretching or ignoring points of law, and that if a matter should give rise to physical conflict, there was no better man to have at your side.

Joshua previewed as best he could from the few details the letter divulged the possibilities of his latest adventure in the 'gun for hire' business. Well, why not, he thought.

19

He'd looked after tenderfeet in the West before. The touring French actress Gisèle Bourdette came to mind. Before that there'd been dime novelist Clem Conway and others. He'd served them all well, though usually the financial reward had barely covered his expenses. Maybe this time would be different. He seemed to recall reading the name Jordan in connection with valuable real estate holdings on Manhattan Island...

It had been arranged that he should rendezvous with Leigh Jordan in a Plains settlement called Greeley, located near the confluence of the Cache La Poudre and South Platte Rivers, a hop, skip and a jump north of the Colorado city of Denver – about eighty miles, he guessed.

Cheyenne, where he would break his rail journey and take the cars for Greeley, was also north of Denver, a matter of 115 miles, and just across the state border in Wyoming. Cheyenne also sat handily as the northern anchor city of the front range of the Rocky Mountains, his and Leigh Jordan's ultimate destination.

In light of his earliness in reaching the region – he was several days ahead of the schedule set out in the letter – Joshua considered whether he should tarry awhile in Cheyenne.

The town hummed, owing its foundation and its prosperity to the railroad. Joshua had heard it called 'the magic city of the Plains'. The railroad gave it direct access to the wider world, and thereby to the latest styles in furniture, the most recently published newspapers and magazines, and the most fashionable apparel from Eastern salons.

But Cheyenne had a rowdy side, too. Not so long ago, in the late 1860s, observers had given the name 'hell-on-wheels' to the throng that had followed the railroad construction gangs across what then had been south-western Dakota Territory.

The word reaching Joshua was that this rough population had encouraged early introduction of the types of rumbustious entertainment commonly associated with the 'Wild West'. Cheyenne had whooped it up, God-forsaken and God-forgotten, with five variety theatres in operation simultaneously. Every other building was a saloon. The shows had regular stages and typically presented what was called burlesque, a saucy relative of legitimate drama featuring female artistes in the skimpiest of dress.

Once, Joshua had seen such a touring 'leg

show' – an imported production performed by a Miss Lydia Thompson and her 'British Blondes'. It was risqué, heady stuff. He wondered whether he might stop to appreciate more of this kind of leg art in Cheyenne.

But on a final analysis, he decided that it might be inadvisable. Not only was he now desperately short of cash, Cheyenne was plumb on the main route from San Francisco. The more miles he could put between himself and the unfortunate incident involving the late Mr Victor Porteous of that city, the better.

He would plunge on into the remoteness of Colorado.

His arrival in Greeley, however, presented Joshua with no further consolation than its comparative isolation. The place was deep in Plains dust and owed the greenness of its fields of tomatoes, melons, cucumbers, potatoes and fruit trees purely to irrigation ditches.

The industrious community had also palisaded itself within a great ring fence, which the free-spirited Joshua regarded with foreboding. Though the place was named after *New York Tribune* editor Horace Greeley, the man who'd exhorted, 'Go West, young man, and grow with the country', Joshua could see little to recommend the township even after being cooped up in a hot and stuffy Denver Pacific Railroad car with a full complement of chewers and spitters.

Grow? In Greeley? A man was more apt to be stifled.

Ah well, at least the great range of the Rocky Mountains looked impressive from here, the blue of storm-clouds, mottled and shadowy, and rising up solidly from the low, still swells of the buff prairie sea against a vivid sky.

Joshua trudged through the coarse granitic dust past scattered frame houses on streets fully a hundred feet wide to a small, rough tavern where he had a room booked in advance by Leigh Jordan.

The host, a dour emigrant from New England, openly disapproved of his early arrival.

'Timetables and written arrangements are meant to be followed, my friend,' he said. 'We stick to such things strictly in the colony here. What will you do with yourself? We have no place for the inefficient, the idle or,' he finished darkly, 'the immoral.'

'I'm sure I can find things to occupy me while I wait for our correspondent from

New York,' Joshua said. 'There must be a bar-room where Greeley citizens sit of an evening and refresh themselves – decorously, of course – after a hard day's toil.'

The tavern keeper was giving him a funny look, but Joshua spoke right on.

'I've a thirst for whiskey right now. Travelling's a dry business.'

The dour host emitted a sound of outrage somewhat like the roar of a wounded grizzly.

'Do you not know our community's first commandment?'

'No,' Joshua said, startled. 'I surely don't. What is it?'

'Thou shalt not sell liquid damnation within the lines of Union Colony.'

Horror! Joshua Dillard figured he must have stranded himself unwittingly in a hotbed of dogmatic intolerance. And as anyone who'd ever had dealings with him would know, he'd be the first person to run foul of narrow-mindedness.

2

TOWN IN A WILD COUNTRY

Temperance was taken to the extreme in Greeley, Joshua learned. A clause in the colony's charter prohibited not just the sale, but also the introduction and consumption of intoxicating liquor.

The good men of Greeley waged their crusade beyond town limits, too. Recently, they'd sacked three houses opened for the sale of liquor near their frontiers. Fine whiskey had been righteously but gleefully poured to waste on the parched desert ground.

As soon as darkness fell, men went to their homes. It was all work and no play. Greeley was abed at an hour when other places were beginning their night's pleasures.

Joshua decided he couldn't abide the 'dry' Greeley for more than one night. Especially after he'd suffered the bugs. They infested the sheets and mattress of his bed. They crawled in swarms seemingly out of the very walls of his room. After he'd been bitten a hundred times, he was forced to leave the bed and doze fitfully on a hard wooden chair till daybreak.

Luckily, salvation was at hand in the form of a freighter passing through the town with a wagon drawn by six mules. At breakfast, swatting away black flies, Joshua raised the subject of the bugs.

The freighter told him the bugs were a persistent pest in Colorado. They came out of the earth and got into the structure of the wooden buildings. Even Greeley cleanliness, which was practised by the women as though a religious virtue, was to no avail.

'The housewives take their beds apart once a week and soak the whole kit and caboodle in carbolic acid. The bugs laugh, I tell yuh,' the freighter said. 'It's best to move on, quick as yuh can.'

So Joshua cadged a ride on his wagon to his (the freighter's) next stop in Fort Harper, a less straitlaced settlement for sure and reputedly with fewer bugs. Moreover, it was another twenty-five miles closer to the Rocky Mountains.

He asked the tavern keeper to pass on a message to Mr Jordan when he arrived, advising him of the change of base and asking him to follow as soon as practicable.

'Greeley is Utopia,' the New Englander said stoutly. 'It's based on religion, temperance and cooperative farming. And are we not entirely free of the universal scourges of crime and laziness? Do you hear ribaldry or profanity? No!'

Joshua shrugged. He didn't want to hear any more of this grave lecture. Nor did he want to argue with the man. 'Let's say it's the bugs and the politics then. I'm too thin-skinned and too liberal in outlook for Greeley.'

Out on the Plains, Joshua spotted from the high seat of the wagon, herds of wild horses, deer, antelope and buffalo.

The freighter had an old Plains rifle stashed under the seat. It was of a type that had succeeded the true Kentucky rifle made the previous century by German gunsmiths in Pennsylvania. Built broadly along similar lines, the freighter's firearm had a stock made to go only halfway up the barrel rather than to the muzzle. The barrel was heavier, purportedly for higher accuracy at longer ranges in open country.

'Good to see you prepared,' Joshua said. 'I hear tell the Indians are raiding in all directions, maddened by the reckless slaughter of the buffalo.'

The freighter scoffed. 'Naw. People always hope to fall in with game is what it is. Every wagoner totes a rifle. Meat and sport are everywhere if you want 'em.'

On this journey, it seemed they didn't.

Fort Harper didn't turn out to be the town of a sybarite's dreams any more than Greeley. But then Joshua hadn't expected or needed that. It was a hotel, a post office, a bank, a livery, two saloons and a scattering of cheerless frame houses; again close to the Cache La Poudre River, like Greeley, but further west and still some fifty miles south of the dubious civilization of Cheyenne.

So far there was no hint of pursuit from San Francisco.

Moreover, Fort Harper survived without the harsh orderliness of Greeley, and with some liquor on hand to ease the discomforts and blind one's eye to the squalor.

Beyond, a low, grassy range called the Foot Hills rose from the Plains.

The town relied on ranching and farming for its trade, and had for a while been a last stop for fur trappers heading into the rugged Rockies – the fast-disappearing mountain men. The 'fort' part suggested a military presence, but Joshua saw no soldiers. Their post, founded ten or some years earlier to protect traders travelling the Overland Trail which passed to the north, was at this date seemingly out of commission.

Joshua took a room at the hotel, surrendered more of his shrunken bill roll, and prepared to take his ease while he awaited the financial relief he hoped would attend the arrival of his client. He washed, shaved and changed into clean clothing.

The hotel was freer of the species of bug that had infested the tavern in Greeley, though it had as many flies. Grasshoppers were Fort Harper's particular bane. Some residents, maybe with Biblical plagues in mind, called them locusts. Threatening crops, they covered the ground and rose with whirring wings most everywhere you walked.

And the people in general were as unlovely as the grasshoppers and the environment in Joshua's estimation.

In the Fort Harper saloons, the locals droned on wholly about dollars and the making of them, usually by 'smart' means, which often meant scoring a trick over a neighbour or friend. According to Fort Harper ethics, this was allowable if not downright applauded.

Still, it suited Joshua a sight better than the contractual goodness of Greeley; he could be more relaxed with the coarse manners, coarse speech, coarse food ... coarse everything. This was a natural order of things to which a hard life had accustomed him.

Two days later, he was propping an elbow on a bar's stained counter and had a boot on its brass rail, pondering how many more drinks he could afford before monetary relief arrived, when he was made keenly aware of another of the saloon's occupants. The fellow was seated, one leg crossed over the other, at a table, smoking a cigar in a superior manner, a man with a cool, detached air, dark, neatly pressed coat and pants, and a linen collar that was spotlessly white above a carefully knotted string tie.

The well-groomed patron was looking him over with thoroughness and distaste, up and down, from top to bottom. He curled a lip and twitched a nostril. A pencil-thin moustache overscored his sneer.

Joshua said, 'Is something bothering you, mister? I ain't partial to being stared at.'

The scrutineer extended a smooth white

hand to point with his cigar; on his little finger a gold signet ring caught the light and glittered. He spat out a flake of loose tobacco from his mouth.

'That tied-down gun, stranger,' he said, indicating the big Peacemaker in the worn holster on Dillard's right thigh. 'Seems well used and well kept. Why, I do believe I see a patina of oil upon it clear across this room. Not a speck of dust or grit, either, I'd judge, which is more than can be said for the rest of your garb.'

Joshua growled. 'Who are you, mister, and what's your point?'

'I'm Walt Sloane and I run the law practice in this burg. You'll find my offices upstairs over the dry-goods store in case you should need to know.'

'Why should I?'

Sloane waved his cigar. 'Oh, legal niceties might be a problem for you sometime.'

'Yeah? How come? I'd think disputes hereabouts would tend to revolve around booze, brawls and bawds rather than points of law.'

'You'd be wrong, stranger. I do quite nicely, helping folks out.'

Doing them down more like, Joshua commented to himself silently. 'And how are you gonna help me?' he said.

'The tied-down gun is the mark of the professional gunfighter. The vigilance committee don't allow shootists in our town. It makes for a bad – uh – atmosphere.'

'Is that right?'

'Yessir. I tell you that for free, without charging a fee. This time, it's on the firm.'

Joshua laughed. 'You hand me any bill, I'd tell you where to stick it, you pompous ass.'

The room, though not crowded, was not empty either, and various drinkers and smokers had ceased their own conversations to eavesdrop on the exchange. Some were boggle-eyed and a few, in the darker corners, tittered at Joshua's sassy retort.

Sloane picked up his empty glass and banged it down three times on the table, angrily. It could have been just a reflex born of frustration at his inability to respond to the belittling insult. It wasn't until a short while later that Joshua realized it had been a signal.

He was reflecting on Sloane's mention of a vigilance committee, and thinking how he didn't much cotton to those entities. Too often he'd found the members were more interested in personal profit than in justice. The committee was a front – a fine pretence

– designed to give respectability to activities more criminal than the wrongs allegedly righted.

Two other drinkers closed in on him at the bar. They were loafer types. He'd seen several of their breed in Fort Harper – hardcase layabouts good only for doing odd jobs. In truth, they were frustrated miners who hadn't hit pay dirt in the mountains during Colorado's gold rushes but had stayed on here because there was nowhere else they wanted to go, nothing else they felt motivated to do.

They had an air of bravado about them. Troublemaking was their intent. Joshua saw it writ large on a face that was pockmarked and smirky, and in another with a silly grin that revealed stained, protruding teeth.

One of the men jostled him to his right, simultaneously apologizing. ''Scuse me, feller. Guess the tanglefoot's made me clumsier than I thought.'

The other man, to his left, meanwhile, stooped and fumbled with something on the floor – a boot-lace maybe – then straightened up.

Seconds after, he nudged Joshua in the ribs. 'Say, what's that yuh got there a-swimming in yore likker? Looks right funny. It a pet o' yore'n?'

Joshua looked. His jaw hardened. One of Fort Harper's pesky, ubiquitous grasshoppers – they were to be discovered even on the saloons' sawdusted floors – was thrashing about in his glass as though trying to keep its head above the amber fluid.

The man on his right started to guffaw and slap his sides. 'Look at this, boys! This stranger's got hisself sump'n better'n a flea circus. Don't some dudes beat all?'

Joshua knew he was being set up, but that didn't stop him. Give him offence and he took the offensive. It was his way.

Keeping his face carefully blank, he hoisted his glass, then with a quick flick of the wrist he sloshed its contents full into the face of the man on his left. It was an imbecile action born of the constant emptiness in his cold heart and the fury in his mind at any kind of victimization.

'No pet of mine, mister. You mightn't have much in the way of brains, but you got it off the floor, remember?'

The man staggered back, clutching at his eyes. 'God a'mighty! Yuh've blinded me, yuh loco bastard!'

A heavy hand fell on Joshua's shoulder, swinging him round. 'That's my pardner's lamps yuh've put out,' said the man from his right. 'I'm gonna bust yuh up.'

Joshua ducked and a ponderous fist hurtled past his ear. 'He brought it on himself. I got no quarrel with you. Let it lie 'less you want a beating.'

'Me, get a beatin'? That's rich from a no-account drifter!'

The ex-miner almost casually threw a second punch. It made glancing contact with Joshua's temple as he dodged the other way, but that was enough to set a fire bell clanging in his head.

Then Joshua's own right fist jabbed out, catching his attacker in the tender part of the neck.

'That'll make the threats stick in your craw,' he taunted.

The man gasped and swore, shaking his great shaggy head. He took a step back, then kicked out brutally with his heavily booted right foot.

Joshua weaved, moved in, shot out both hands and grabbed the thug's leg. He got a grip on the kneecap. He twisted hard.

The man snorted with the tearing pain of it; foul breath hissed past Joshua's ear as he swayed and fought to keep balance on his left leg.

Suddenly relinquishing his hold, Joshua shot up a piledriver punch almost from the floor which caught the tottering ex-miner under the bracket of his chin. It was an incredibly powerful blow. The miner was lifted off his feet and sent flying backwards across the saloon. When his heels hit the floor, he carried on stumbling backwards till he crashed into an upright Hawkins piano, transported to Fort Harper at considerable expense from Philadelphia.

The saloon's prized possession collapsed under his weight and velocity. Panels splintered, keys flew, wires sprung – all amidst a great cacophony of unmusical sound and mingled shouts of encouragement, excitement, shock and dismay.

And it wasn't over yet.

The troublemaker who'd received Joshua's drink in his face had managed to wipe the stinging liquor out of reddened eyes and was ready to exact retribution.

Another big man, he lunged at Joshua, swinging a right fist that was like a ham. Joshua stepped inside, landing a well-aimed left on his nose. He felt a satisfying crunch as the misshapen nose, broken in some earlier fight, gave under the blow. Blood erupted.

'Don't push me any further,' Joshua warned, 'or I'll put you out cold like your friend.'

But he wasn't heeded. 'The hell you say! I'm gonna kill yuh!'

The blood streaming down his shirt and vest, the grasshopper prankster came back, both arms wind-milling. One of his mighty fists caught Joshua in the eye.

It was a fight neither was prepared to call off. Moments later, they lost their footing. They'd been standing wide-legged in the middle of the room, exchanging ferocious punches, toe to toe. The roughneck threw a punch that failed to connect. When he tumbled forward with its unchecked impetus, he carried Joshua with him and they ended up in a rolling heap in the sawdust.

The ex-miner, coming out on top, got astride Joshua and pinned him face down by his sheer weight. He lifted his fist to deliver a rabbit punch to the nape of Joshua's neck.

Joshua heard his rasping intake of breath and guessed what was coming. He knew that if the blow landed it could snap the top of his spine, killing him.

He heaved up his body mightily with all that was left of the strength in his arms and legs, unseating the man from his arching back like a bucking bronc. The punch whistled past his ear and smashed into the hard floor.

The man gasped, rose to his knees, threw back his head and seized his badly jarred wrist, all in automatic reaction. For a moment his rearing body was uncovered.

Scrambling to his feet first, Joshua kicked him in the midriff. His boot found soft tissue and sank deep.

The ex-miner went over backwards, his face turning the grey of putty. His mouth dropped open breathlessly and vomit gushed out in a vile stream specked with blood.

A stunned hush, interspersed by a groan or two of disgust, spread through the saloon. And the barkeep intervened, producing a menacing shotgun.

'Right, fellers. That's more than plenty. There's damage done. Who's gonna pay?'

Joshua wiped his bleeding, teeth-cut lips and squinted through his rapidly closing hit eye at Walt Sloane.

'It's him I blame,' he said, nodding at the attorney. 'He was back of this trouble.'

Despite his vision not being its best, Joshua reckoned Sloane was seething at the vanquishing of his two bully-boys, though he managed to mask it with a cool, detached air. He exhaled a cloud of cigar smoke, rubbed out the butt, which he tossed in the direction of a malodorous spittoon, and spread his empty hands.

'I don't see how,' he said, all innocence. 'The boys were funning and misjudged your temper is all.'

'Is that so, Mr Sloane? Well, I reckon they set about me for money, not for fun. Or punishment. Tell 'em don't ever force me to fight again if they don't like the way I fight.'

'Hardly my business,' Sloane said, with a careless shrug. 'Mind if I ask your name, seeing as you have mine?'

'Name's Dillard.'

'I take it you have some affairs in Fort Harper.'

'Yeah, and I'll be minding 'em my ownself.'

'I only wanted to help. You're a hard man, Mr Dillard.'

'It's a hard country, Mr Sloane.'

The grey-faced grasshopper impresario was still making wet, whistling sounds in his throat as he fought to regain his breath.

3

CROSSING JORDAN

The timing of the encounter in the saloon proved especially unfortunate. Joshua made tracks for the hotel to clean up the results of the fight, and he reached it coincidentally with the arrival of the stage-wagon from Greeley as dusk was falling.

A woman passenger was being helped down the steps by the Jehu, who showed her much deference and respect. She was a woman in or approaching her forties and no longer a young beauty. But she still cut a splendid figure in a matching dark-blue bonnet and travelling cape. In her descent, she lifted her ruffled skirt and petticoat to reveal shapely calves. The sight made Joshua acutely alive to the likelihood that a similar fullness and splendour of the flesh might be discovered in other parts of her curvaceous anatomy.

In her maturity, the stage passenger had preserved the pulse-quickening allure of a woman in her twenties. For Joshua, accustomed to Western women of similar age who'd lost their looks to drudgery, child-bearing and sicknesses in harsh environments, she was an exciting sight he'd not expected in these parts.

He followed her into the lobby where he found her already in conversation with the landlord.

She turned, no doubt expecting to see one of the stage line people bringing in a valise or carpetbag. She recoiled, affronted by what she beheld.

'My God!' she said to the landlord. 'Is this fellow a guest here, too?'

The landlord lowered his eyes in confusion and shuffled his feet. 'Er, yes, ma'am, I guess he is.'

She took off her bonnet, shaking out lustrous chestnut tresses in which Joshua could see not a trace of grey. 'A common ruffian. His clothes are filthy and smell of spilt liquor,' she commented under her breath.

Joshua overheard, as indeed he thought he was meant to. But he was not shamed, if that was what the woman intended.

'I regret my appearance doesn't meet with your approval, ma'am.' He brushed sawdust from his sleeves and pants legs. 'But in point of fact I'm growing a mite tired of folks judging my dress, so I'll not apologize.'

She huffed. 'It's more than dress. Who gave you the black eye?'

'No one gave it me, ma'am. I got it in trade for bloody noses and sore bodies and dazed heads.'

'I thought so. A drunken brawler,' she accused.

The landlord cut in, trying to avert what was developing into a clash between his guests. 'There won't be any disturbances in this hotel, Mrs Jordan, but I'm afraid Fort Harper is a far piece from New York City and no place for a lady.'

Joshua turned to the landlord, fixing him with his good eye. 'Did you say Jordan? Is Mr Jordan with this lady?'

The landlord was flummoxed, but the woman came to his rescue.

'Mr Jordan is nowhere, unless you count in a coffin six feet underground,' she said. Her voice was blunt and emotionless.

'You mean Jordan is dead?' Joshua asked her.

'Six months departed from the vale of tears,' she said sardonically.

'But I have letters from Leigh Jordan written this past month!'

'I'm Leigh Jordan. Mrs Leigh Jordan. And I take it that you must be Mr Joshua Dillard, whom I've foolishly engaged for my guidance and protection.'

Joshua's aching head spun. The person who'd hired him was a woman – this woman!

He strived to look indignant at her insults, though he was all too aware that this was impossible with bruised, blotched, swollen and bloodied features.

'Foolishly, ma'am?' he intoned through split lips.

'I was misinformed, sir. You've the appearance of a broken-down bum, whereas your services were recommended by one of the nation's foremost detective agencies.'

Joshua gave mental thanks to his Pinkerton contacts, and to her indiscretion in mentioning them and giving him his opening.

The landlord's ears were nigh on flapping.

'Ah,' Joshua said. 'No doubt it was for some unconventional matter the agency weren't prepared to handle themselves. Maybe you've gotten in mind doing something that ain't strictly legal-like...'

His shot in the dark had the effect he desired.

She stiffened. 'We'll not discuss this until I'm settled in my room. You may visit me privately.'

Accordingly, the discussion was resumed after supper in the mettlesome lady's upstairs chamber. Joshua looked around as he entered. It was twice the size of his own room and had one large double bed. Two china bowls with pitchers sat on a low, mirrored washstand with folded towels beside them.

'Ma'am,' he began, 'I'm sorry to hear about your husband.' Though not in the best of moods, he'd cleaned up some and meant to start on a fresh foot, observing the proprieties.

Leigh Jordan had contrary ideas.

'You needn't be,' she said. 'Humphrey Jordan was an old man. Very old, and I'd been married to him for only a few years. We'll be honest from the outset. I married him for security and comfort, name and money, when I became too old for a life that demands more of a mature woman than it's wise to give. Old Man Jordan had an attractive trinket for his house and his arm, not to mention more intimate matters, and he was satisfied with the bargain.'

'He was a real-estate man, wasn't he?'

44

'One of the smartest. He had some of the richest holdings in New York City, but the secret of his success was to continually broaden the base of his investments. As his widow, I'm the stewardess of his wealth. I believe I'm his match in business acumen and intend to further his principles, which is why you and I are here.'

Joshua frowned. 'I didn't know that was so, exactly. I'm not a financially savvy man.'

'No, of course not,' Leigh snapped. 'You're some kind of bounty hunter.'

Joshua held up open hands toward her. 'Nor that either.'

She snorted. 'Well, you're ruthless, which is what I want. Gun-handy and able to function as my bodyguard – a guide and an escort all in one.'

'Maybe I can be that,' Joshua said, nodding. 'But I ain't a native to this country. A man who is would have an edge on me. He'd know of trails and places of concealment of which I could know nothing. In some situations, such as if you have an enemy or competitor, that advantage might mean the difference between life and death.'

Leigh thought on it, then said, 'But you're the kind of man a lone woman must have in wild country. A mercenary.'

'I sometimes call myself a soldier of fortune,' Joshua said tentatively.

Her lips curved as she regarded again his battered visage and his hastily brushed, shabby clothing.

'A soldier of misfortune, I'd say. It's your appearance and your careless resort to violence that perturb me. Also, it was high-handed of you to change my arrangements and shift here from Greeley. Everything in this place is thick with black flies and jumping with grasshoppers. I've seen it already. Supper was dreadful.'

'Do tell.'

'I will. The beef was tough, the butter had turned to oil, and both were black with half-drowned flies. The tablecloth was grease-stained and swarming with more of them.'

Joshua wasn't wearing her complaints. 'If you'd stayed in Greeley, you'd have seen there were as many flies. Worse, you'd have been chewed up something awful by bed bugs. If you don't like my decisions, maybe we'd better go our separate ways.'

Calculatedly, he was calling her bluff.

Something that might have been alarm flitted across Leigh's even features. She sighed. 'Well, I must allow that cleaned up a piece you do look less broken-down and less

46

of a bum. And a man with some brutality in him might be what I'll need.'

'My brutality has saved the lives of clients more than once.'

'But your prior fight here is regrettable and would never have happened if you'd stayed in Greeley.'

She stood up, as though reaching a final decision and declaring a truce. 'Come here, over by the washbowl. Take off your coat. I've some iodine in my kit and that eye still needs attention.'

Well, if she wanted to make amends for her rudeness, far be it for him to reject them. And he didn't really want to walk out of Fort Harper more empty-handed than he'd arrived.

Leigh Jordan ran a suddenly moist tongue over her dry lips. With his coat off, she could see for certainty that Joshua Dillard was a big man of rangy build, broad and muscular in the shoulders, slim in the waist and flank. He also had a lean, brown face and eyes blue and clear.

As well as his other potential uses to her, she realized that he was the type of powerful and arousing man to whom, when she'd been a working girl, she'd never had any reservations about selling her favours. Pleasure (her own) as well as profit had entered into the equation with such men.

She poured iodine from a small brown bottle onto a lace-fringed handkerchief and dabbed at the splits on his face. He winced.

'Does it sting?' she asked needlessly.

'I can stand it,' he said.

She dabbed some more, thought some more, all the time her hands growing a little unsteadier. It was a long time since she'd touched flesh and had it produce this effect on her. Frankly, it was a sensation she could admit to herself that she'd missed, despite the hypocritical morality of her time.

'There, it's done now.'

On an impulse, she bent forward and put her lips to his sore mouth.

He was surprised, but responded as she'd known he would. Then she answered his kiss with an ardour he'd clearly not expected.

When eventually they let their lips part for breath, she said, 'You must be shocked at me.'

'Nope. You're a woman still in her prime. Nature and instincts will rule a being, male or female, anytime.'

She said huskily, 'Joshua – I may call you that, mayn't I? I'm a woman deprived by circumstances of things which were once familiar and a solace to her. Brought together as we are, at the end of nowhere and with only strangers inside gossiping distance, wouldn't it be silly for us to ignore that this room and its bed were made for two?'

4

RUNAWAY

By the first roseate light of a new day, filtered through the bedroom curtains, Joshua Dillard had even more reason to be in a better mood than when he'd first encountered a disapproving Leigh Jordan.

She, too, showed no remorse about the way they'd spent her first night in Fort Harper; no post-coital tears, or the irrational tantrums that a younger, less-experienced woman might have thrown. Not that Joshua had expected any, but he was glad of her plain good sense.

Leigh affected no coyness either. More than accepting his knowledge of her sensuality, she paraded it before him. She went about the room naked, easing the kinks from sleep-stiffened muscles with gentle exercises before going to the washstand and performing the most intimate ablutions in front of the mirror and in his full view.

Joshua appreciated the all-revealing double image of her, front and back. She had a body any mature woman could be proud of, and she clearly wasn't ashamed of it. Generously rounded in the buttocks and thighs; full and heavy, but not pendulous, in the breasts.

It was hard for him to hold in check his hunger for her soft red lips, her responsive brown nipples, the primed notch between her legs. He was ready to take her again.

But first he had to find out her other secrets. She wanted his professional services. For what exactly? A niggle at the back of his mind said something didn't fit quite square. His life had taught him at high cost a degree of caution – which was a hard-earned quality for one naturally inclined to recklessness. Caution told him a man needed to tread careful-like when a handsome woman threw herself at his head.

'Leigh...' he ventured. 'I guess we've strayed from our original intentions, and

I've no complaint on that score. Last night was a joy I'd not expected. Yet you must tell me more about the investment business you have in this country, and how I can help you with it.'

'Oh, Joshua,' she teased. 'How can you talk about business? I think I must have drained your fountain.'

He laughed. 'I'm sure tempted to prove you wrong there. Howsoever, you've irons in your fire of another kind and it'd be selfish of me to ignore that. They might get cold.'

She grew serious and picked up a robe which she pulled around her. 'Yes ... I was just thinking the very same thing myself. Lying together is nice, but I mustn't let myself be too carried away.'

'Me neither. I took it you were planning to ride into mountain country,' Joshua prompted.

'I think the sooner we do so the better. Today I'll want you to go to the livery and choose suitable mounts for us that I can rent or buy. We might also need a little food and equipment.'

'What will we be doing in the mountains?'

'The high country valleys, or "parks" as they call them here, have a huge potential

51

which few have yet recognized. The Ute and Arapahoe tribes are believed to have made these places a prime hunting ground, rich in game of many kinds. I want to use wealth I've inherited from Humphrey to buy up a valley and turn it into a hunting refuge for rich foreigners – aristocrats and such – and Eastern businessmen. I'll have a hotel, lodges, cabins...'

A gleam entered Leigh's eyes. 'In years to come, I'm sure my scheme will repay the investment a thousandfold.'

'Could be right,' Joshua said, though with much less enthusiasm. 'Yet I seem to remember the Homestead Act kind of precluded one person from holding more than a hundred and sixty acres.'

'Fiddlesticks! There are ways round that. First off, the deeds can be transferred to what I believe are known as dummy entry-men – loafers, drifters, even the deceased. Then I'll buy the land from these new owners, paying the government a small fee, and registering a corporation to run the park.'

Joshua considered, then shook his head. 'Don't sound too legal. What if the settlers and ranchers now in possession oppose your ideas?'

'I'm sure a capable man like yourself could make them see sense,' she said.

'Maybe so, maybe not. This will need some thinking over. But I'll tell you straight, I ain't sure I cotton to harassing honest folks.'

Leigh lifted her queenly head. 'Well, I do hope you think quickly. After breakfast, I propose you find us those horses.'

'No harm in riding out apiece and testing the climate of opinion, I guess.'

'Good,' Leigh said. 'For now our deal stands then. I'm glad.'

But she said it through tight lips.

The Fort Harper livery had passable horse-flesh for rent and Joshua picked out three animals – one for a pack-horse – that he judged would meet their requirements. The liveryman told him the chestnut was an especially gentle animal, and its attractive colour put Joshua in mind of Leigh Jordan's hair, which he now knew to be wholly natural.

All the same, returning from the stable, he didn't recognize Leigh at first when he almost passed her in the street. She was wearing a calfskin vest over a white, frilled blouse and her long, shapely legs were shown off rather than concealed by tailored corduroy pants and tooled leather half-boots.

Joshua arched his eyebrows. 'You sure make a fine sight for the Fort Harper citizenry,' he complimented her.

'What these folk think doesn't rate with me – I don't give a damn,' she said.

'Too right you don't,' Joshua said with a laugh.

'What does matter though is that I've discovered this two-bit burg boasts its own lawyer.'

Joshua groaned. 'You mean Walt Sloane?'

Leigh looked surprised. 'Why, yes, I do. I've spoken with him in his office up those stairs beside the dry-goods store. I've made a further appointment with him where he can allay your misgivings about my visionary plans, and he'll facilitate contacts with landowners...' She trailed off. 'What's wrong?'

'I don't know that's the best way to go about things. I reckon Sloane's no more'n a shyster. I wouldn't trust him, were I–'

He was about to explain his view when a developing situation outside the town's general store grabbed his attention and he stopped. A small buckboard, to which was harnessed a single black mare, was drawn up there on the main drag. A girl had been carrying out, piecemeal, various purchases to load the tray.

She was a plain-looking youngster. She might have seen some fifteen summers, was sturdy in limb and dressed in rough grey homespun. Not lovely, but with clean, dark hair and a blooming figure that not even her shapeless dress could conceal. All this Joshua had noted casually at an earlier cursory glance. Probably she was a hardworking rancher's girl sent to town to collect the week's bought supplies and other sundries.

What interested him now was that she was receiving the humiliating attention of the very same pair of loafers who'd bothered him at Sloane's behest the day before. He'd since learned their names were Buck Borden and Chaz Clancey, but he recognized them by the marks of their bruising encounter if nothing else. Standing across the street, they were calling out ribald remarks, causing the girl to blush and her dark eyes to flash.

'Yore Bible-thumpin' paw let yuh *con-sort* with woman-starved fellers, gal?' one loafer called.

'Aw, she's too sweet an' good to lift her thick skirt, pard!'

'Bet she ain't got no dainty things to wear

under it neither. Yuh think mebbe she jest goes about *bare-assed?*'

Worse, they started to toss pebbles at the patient mare.

Leigh asked, 'What are you staring at, Joshua?'

'Wait a moment, Leigh. I'm gonna stop those galoots. For certain sure, they didn't learn their lesson yesterday.'

Leigh took a brief look. She expelled a ragged sigh of annoyance. 'Oh, leave it, can't you? The hicks' crude funning and their prissy little she-noodle are none of our concern.'

Suddenly, the mare, stung on the rump by a pebble, whinnied and half-reared. The girl in grey cried, 'Whoa, Sally!'

But as soon as scrabbling forefeet hit the ground, raising a blinding cloud of dust, another pebble found its target, and the spooked horse took off at a gallop. The buckboard hurtled along behind, jolting and banging and shedding items of its load onto the street.

A big, bearded man with a patch over his left eye came out of a barbershop, face still lathered, followed by a fierce-looking dog. 'Go, Felicity, go!' he roared. 'Stop 'er, gal!'

But Joshua could see the heavy-skirted

Felicity didn't have a prayer. As horse and buckboard swerved round a corner into a cross street, he weighed up whether he should commandeer a mount from the nearest hitch rail and give chase to the runaway.

Horseman that he was, among many other things, he decided against it. Pursuit wasn't the best idea. Horses were both herd and prey animals. They had the flight instinct. Another horse pounding after Felicity's mare would only make the panicky creature run even faster.

The best course was to run along behind on foot. If the buckboard stayed attached, the horse would be pretty much dragged to a halt anyway. Then he could just move in and grab the harness.

Joshua put his swift thoughts into action. Turning the corner, he was in time to see a front wheel run plumb into a pothole and the buckboard heel over onto its side.

That brought the horse to a sort of standstill, prancing on the spot, turning back as though looking to see what it was that had scared her. In fact, she'd run less than a couple of hundred yards. When Joshua stepped up, she rolled her eyes with a protesting snort. She shied away and side-stepped, stiff-legged.

Joshua seized the broken harness to hold her in place. She whickered as he began talking quietly and soothingly. 'Quiet, gal, ain't nobody throwing another goddamn thing at you. We won't let 'em.'

The mare tried to rear again, uncertain of his strange touch and the swirling dust. But the dust quickly settled, and he'd yanked her down onto all fours and was patting her again before Felicity joined them and began rubbing her gently on the muzzle, neck and shoulder, talking kindly nonsense.

The horse was finally quietened.

'Thanks, mister,' the girl said.

'Kinda skittish, is she?'

'No, mister. You saw. It was just them fellers, throwing stuff. Sally ain't skittish at all. My pa'll skin me when he learns about this.'

The tawny-bearded, eye-patched man came loping up, dog frisking at his heels. 'Goddamn – beggin' your absent pa's pardon, Miss Felicity – I ain't never seen Carver Elliot's mare do such a thing afore.'

'Strange animals, horses, and every one different,' Joshua said. 'I had a ninety-five per cent calm horse who died real young coupla years back. He was sometimes startled by absolutely nothing ... like spring daffodils nodding in the breeze. This one did have an excuse, however.'

'It was those bully-boys who hang about lawyer Sloane's place, Hank,' Felicity said, and she explained about the calling-out and pebble-throwing. Then names were exchanged and sketchy introductions made.

Felicity Elliot was the daughter of small rancher Carver Elliot. She lived with him and her stepmother 'up the valley'. The Elliots were 'a very God-fearing family'.

Hank Montgomery was a hunter and trapper better known as 'Mountain Hank' and he had a squatter's claim a much further piece up the same valley. His wolfish dog was Hornet. They largely shunned society, but he'd been in town 'on a spree'.

Joshua said little beyond acknowledging he was a stranger hereabouts, staying at the hotel.

'How say we put the rig back on its wheels, and oblige the hoodlums to reload it and shell out for spoiled goods?' he asked.

Mountain Hank approved. 'Bet your sweet life we'll do just that.'

Beneath the tall mountain man's scruffy hunting suit was a powerful physique that might have enabled him to right the buckboard single-handed. Despite his rough speech, he had chivalrous manners and his eye patch gave him a romantic, piratical air. In fact, Joshua considered him a mite theatrical.

Hornet was a mongrel – part wolf, part Alsatian – and totally attentive to his master.

The buckboard serviceable again, they went in search of the two bothersome ex-miners, Borden and Clancey. They found them, loafing in the sun as largely was their wont, he suspected, outside a saloon.

The pair visibly trembled in their boots, faced with the combined wrath of two men who matched them for weight and surpassed them in determination. Joshua Dillard had proven himself a scant seventeen hours before; Mountain Hank had a longer-standing local reputation.

'We was jest joshin' the kid,' Clancey said. 'No harm were intentioned.'

'Sure am glad to hear it, fellers,' said Joshua. ''Cause you're gonna pick up Miss Elliot's stuff that's fallen in the street and put it back on her buckboard. Anything that's busted up bad you're gonna replace.'

As they gathered up the last of Felicity's scattered goods, Leigh Jordan joined Joshua and Felicity on the plankwalk outside the general store. Joshua sensed Leigh was back in her prickliest mood.

'Miss Elliot – Mrs Leigh Jordan, of New York City,' he said with an open gesture of each hand in turn.

Felicity took in the stylish vest and the unmarked new corduroy pants. She swept back her dark hair with a nervous hand, but her open face beamed with pleasure and she made a half-curtsy. 'Always nice to meet a real lady, Mrs Jordan. We don't get too many about Fort Harper.'

Her smile gave an unusual, distinctive twist to her lips which Joshua found quite charming.

But Leigh Jordan froze. For some reason Joshua couldn't fathom, she was suddenly more than piqued. She turned her back on Felicity's smile and said, 'Mr Dillard, I made it plain I didn't want you embroiling yourself in any more squabbles with local people. You hired out to me.'

'But that don't mean I have to seek your nod for everything I do.' He shook his head in puzzlement. Over-reaction was supposedly *his* flaw. 'It's ridiculous, Leigh. Why, next thing you'd have me asking permission to shoo the flies away!'

Leigh stamped a foot. 'Last night, Joshua, I thought we'd reached an understanding.'

'Well, what happened did seem a mighty fine outcome at the time.'

'Today, all you've done is raise petty objections and fool around chasing after a runaway horse that had nothing to do with us. Consider our arrangement dissolved forthwith! I shall go into partnership with Mr Sloane.'

5

MOUNTAIN HANK GETS MAD

Joshua's jaw dropped. 'That rattlesnake! Of all the chuckleheaded ideas... Act like you had some good sense, Leigh.'

'I will. Walt Sloane thinks my scheme is a crackerjack.'

Joshua was staggered. A partnership with the likes of Walt Sloane would mean having to share the profits of the venture. He'd no doubt of that. Surely Leigh Jordan could see it, too. Why should she want to throw in with anyone, let alone a tricky lawyer? In Joshua's line of work, surprises came ten a penny. But this one floored him.

If he'd lost her commission, and the money she'd been going to pay him, Sloane had already gotten him (Joshua) in a bind. With his 'crackerjack' flattery, the lawyer had won Leigh over apparently and managed to do him out of her confidence. How long would it be before he twisted her?

'A partnership, eh?' Joshua said. 'All right, have it your own way. Who pays my hotel bill? I'm about cleaned out and I don't fancy offering to chop wood to clear the debt.'

'I'll pay, straight away. But consider you have notice to vacate the room as of now.' Leigh turned heel and headed off to the hotel, head erect, spine stiff and without a backward glance.

'Obliged,' Joshua called after her, not meaning it. 'Unbelievable...' he said, under his breath.

Felicity, who'd been listening agape, said, 'Seems like I've gotten you into some kinda trouble, Mr Dillard.'

'Must've been going to happen anyhow, young lady.'

She hung her head and shuffled her feet. 'I feel real bad about it. What can I do?'

'Go ahead home – you don't owe anything to anybody.'

'But you said you had no money. Where will you stay?'

Joshua shrugged. 'Something'll turn up. I'm used to making do, and I do hear tell you can sleep out of doors in Colorado for six months of the year.'

He wasn't exaggerating to make her feel less uncomfortable. The plains' altitude was 4,000 to 6,000 feet. Some of the settled parks or valleys were even higher – 8,000, 10,000 feet. The air was rarefied and dry; rainfall way below average; dews rare; fogs rarer yet. And Joshua was a western man and accustomed to coping with a wilderness life as circumstances dictated.

Mountain Hank, reeking incongruously of fancy toilet water, returned from the barbershop, beard and hair trimmed, in time to catch the drift of the conversation.

'Why, Felicity, don't your pa take in the odd boarder come into the country on account of their health?' he asked.

It was common knowledge that the climate of Colorado was considered the best in North America for consumptives, asthmatics, dyspeptics and sufferers from nervous disabilities. Thousands came trying the 'camp cure' or settling permanently. Sixty-eight miles south of Denver, the eccentric but far-sighted General William Jackson Palmer, a railroad entrepreneur, had founded his Fountain Colony which was quickly becoming a mecca for the victims of respiratory diseases.

'But I'm no invalid,' Joshua said.

Felicity came over shy and awkward, as though she didn't know what she should say.

Hank said, 'When parties camp in the canyon, he sells milk and butter to 'em, too, does your pa.'

'Sure he does, Hank,' Felicity returned, 'but it's a fair ride into wild country. Mr Dillard might not want to be so isolated. Besides, Pa will insist an able-bodied man make himself agreeable, doing hard chores and the like. It's a spell ago since the last time he took in a fit feller, and he charged that one five dollars a week to boot.'

'I own your pa drives a hard bargain an' it ain't no room in a fine boardin'-house,' Hank said. 'Just a leaky old shack alongside your house, but Joshua here ain't in a position to be too damn' particular.'

'That I'm not,' Joshua said.

Felicity gave him the unplanned treat of one of her individual smiles. 'Then what do you say, Mr Dillard?'

'If that's an invitation, I'd be a fool to pass

it up. Maybe I'll go with you so I can discuss it with your father.'

The decision made, Joshua fetched his bag from the hotel, and Mountain Hank went with Hornet – who barked excitedly at the prospect of the run home – to mount a large-boned, heavy-hooved sorrel horse tied at the rail outside the barbershop. It was all of eighteen hands and he needed a mount that size.

Minutes later, they were riding out of Fort Harper, Joshua on the buckboard's bench alongside Felicity.

All the while, Joshua pondered Leigh Jordan's abrupt change of heart. He could come up with no answers, and it niggled him like an itch he couldn't scratch.

The ascent over grassy hills into the upland park followed no real road and they met no other travellers. The sky was blue and the air hot and still. Joshua had seen much of the Western states and territories, but he was awed by the beauty of the country.

They forded a river fed by the snows that brilliantly capped the higher purple peaks in the ranges beyond. Fish leaped high from the water, sunlight catching the silver of their arcing bodies. Here and there were breaks in the smooth hills in the shape of walls and terraces of multi-hued rock, weathered and stained by ores. It was a stunning landscape.

Once, passing through a headily scented wood of pitch-pine and spruce, an elk with branched horns spreading a good three feet lifted its huge head and stared at them before Hornet, stalking up on the creature with ridiculous bravado, abandoned his stealth and went to barking. Unconcernedly, the monster trotted briskly away and was lost from sight. Mountain Hank called Hornet to heel. The trees were alive with birds and the clamour interrupted their songs. Joshua saw several pairs of crested blue jays take wing.

'It's a paradise for big game,' Hank said to Joshua. 'Wait till you see the deer, bighorn, mountain cats, grizzlies...'

'Oh, yes, big game,' Joshua said. 'That was the attraction for Mrs Leigh Jordan.'

Hank jerked in his saddle in surprise; the leather creaked under his great weight. 'What! That city woman! Was she a *hunter*?'

Joshua grinned. 'Rest easy, friend. I reckon no. But she's got this smart plan for buying up the Indians' old hunting-grounds – this entire valley – and setting up a resort where she can fleece her rich friends from back

East. She'll prob'ly be making an offer for your place and Mr Elliot's hundred-and-sixty.'

This time Hank leaped as though a fire-cracker had exploded under his nose. He rose in his stirrups with such a roar, Joshua was surprised his mighty mount stayed placid.

'By God!' he raged. 'Nobody buys my claim. I've a good mind to ride back to Fort Harper an' tell that fancy New Yorker she can get to hell out of it!'

'I tried to point out there might be other views on the matter myself,' Joshua said. 'But she had some sorta confabulation with Walt Sloane. He agreed to back her play, so now she won't listen.'

'Sloane's a crook – ever'body knows that! Pure poison. Lookit the way he manipulates them miner fellers.'

'No question about that.'

'An' that ain't the half of it. Was Sloane behind the vigilance committee, a fine name for "Judge Lynch" and a few feet of rope. Him a lawyer, too – the mangy coyote! For two pins, I'd tear out his guts.'

Felicity was beginning to look alarmed at the increasing violence of Mountain Hank's utterances. His one eye was glittering madly.

'Hank, you mustn't get steamed up so. It does you no good.'

Hank snarled, 'Where d'you get off tellin' me what to do, gal? You're startin' to sound like your Godbotherin' pa!'

Joshua said in a firm and even voice, 'You know better how to mind your manners, Mr Montgomery. Miss Elliot meant no offence. She had your own best interests in mind, I'm sure.'

'Waal, that's as maybe,' Hank said, but with less than perfect grace. 'Gotta leave you folks here anyways. Felicity's all right, but Carver Elliot don't see eye to eye with me nohow. Never has. Me an' Hornet'll go on up to my place by the back trails.'

He whistled the dog and gigged his horse into motion, and then a canter, leaving the buckboard behind. Going at speed, he cut a dangerous, ruffianly figure, the butts of two pistols sticking out from his belt.

Joshua arched his eyebrows. 'What was that all about?'

'Pa and Hank and Hornet are old enemies,' Felicity said. 'It's best they avoid each other's company.'

'Tell me more,' Joshua prompted.

'The truth of it is they're as like as chalk and cheese. Pa puts the words of his Bible first and foremost. Mountain Hank respects nothing, specially not Pa's religion. He's a man of fight and swagger whose season has passed, I guess.'

'He sure looks like an old-time desperado, eye patch and all. How did he lose an eye?'

'That was a she-bear he disturbed with her cubs. But one time he was an army scout and he fought against Indians in frontier wars. He's a very brave and good man, I'm sure, but awful prone to moodiness and strange sorrows. He has also gotten a fondness for redeye whiskey. The anger you saw is nothing. Sometimes when he goes on the spree, he drinks too much liquor and gets really scary. Pa calls Hank's terrible tempers his "ugly fits" and says the Devil is in him. He also says Hornet is a devil-dog.'

'Worrying,' Joshua said, thinking more of the two pistols and the mad glitter in the mountain man's eye.

'Well, don't tell my pa that he was there in town today to help us. I'm glad, though. Hank's powerful good at righting buckboards.'

'Powerful is the word.'

Felicity put Sally onto a definite track by the side of a rushing stream. Or the horse took it out of long habit, Joshua didn't quite know which.

They were unmistakably in mountain country with the pine-scattered slopes rising steeply around them. A primitive bridge of lashed logs covered with pine bark took them across the stream. 'Not far now,' Felicity said.

Into sight among some cottonwoods came a good-sized log cabin with a flat mud roof. A long, ramshackle barn, two corrals and a smaller cabin made up the ranch buildings.

Higher up stood a simple sawmill, putting to use the valuable water power of the fast-flowing stream. Logs were piled about, evidence that Carver Elliot operated his holding as a lumberman as well as a rancher. A crib dam of interlocking timbers filled with stones created a pond above the mill, storing water and effectively increasing the flow.

A tall, thin man with a stoop, dressed in severely impractical black smock and trousers to which clung bits of straw and dirt, came from the barn to meet them. This, murmured Felicity, was her pa, Carver Elliot. There was no point of likeness between them, so Joshua assumed the girl must favour her dead mother. The man's careworn face was pinched, gaunt and sallow; his welcome hostile.

'What possesses you, child?' the man demanded austerely. 'You know we've no time for entertaining strangers. And by what right, sir, are you in the unchaperoned company of my daughter – a decent, respectable girl brung up according to teachings inspired by our Master? I forbid this corrupting impropriety – 'tis an affront, an offence in the eyes of the good Lord!'

None of Elliot's stern harangue boded well.

Joshua realized his time alone with Felicity could have been more wisely spent. He should have been quizzing her about her own folks instead of learning the sad history of Mountain Hank.

6

SIN DESTROYER

'Are you a minister of religion, Mr Elliot?'

Joshua, Felicity and Carver Elliot had gone into the parlour of the big cabin. Small windows of poorly made glass, full of flaws and whorls, let daylight reveal a bare, boarded floor, a rough stone fireplace, a carpet-covered backwoods couch, and an empty table with tall, straight-backed chairs.

'No, Mr Dillard, I am not. There is no minister in these parts.' Elliot drew himself up to his fullest height. 'But you don't have to wear the cloth to recognize sin and be its destroyer.'

From the shadows, his second wife, who wore a drab grey dress similar to Felicity's but didn't have any of the girl's shapeliness to fill it, fixed Joshua with pale-blue eyes. Words issued in a whine from her lipless mouth.

'Carver is a man of strong convictions and provides all the guidance needed under this roof. The Lord spared him from the consumption to save us.'

'I thought He sent someone else to do that,' Joshua said.

Mrs Elliot, a sourpuss with no sense of humour, explained, 'In Illinois, Carver was brought to death's door. Here, the Lord has repaired his health, hallelujah! In His wisdom, He must have had a good reason.'

'Yeah, the same reason He had for giving the Colorado mountain valleys dry and rarefied air, I guess.'

The rejoinder was too deep for Mrs Elliot, as Joshua had known it would be. She retired from the conversation in deference to her husband with whom Joshua discussed the mundane details of his possible accommodation. He dodged mentioning that he didn't currently have the funds to cover more than one week's five-dollar charge, and confirmed he 'would make himself agreeable' doing manual tasks.

The deal struck didn't placate the surly puritan altogether. His eyes dwelled on how Joshua wore his gunbelt, how the holster was cut away around the Peacemaker's trigger-guard, and how the holster was tied to his thigh with a leather thong.

'Vengeance is the Lord's,' he said. 'There'll be no using your weapon here, Mr Dillard. Just honest toil.'

Although Elliot intended to take every advantage of Joshua as unpaid labour, Felicity remained under a dark cloud for the unseemly manner in which she'd brought Joshua to his doorstep. Plainly, the hypocrisy escaped him.

'The whole thing was the fault of the loafers in Fort Harper,' Joshua tried to tell him.

Which only exacerbated matters.

'Then I fear the child has become the Devil's tool and stirred the lust in men's loins,' Elliot said. The gleam of a fanatic was in his eyes. 'Bring me the Bible, woman, we must beg forgiveness for the child.'

Joshua protested mildly. 'Aw, c'mon, Mr Elliot. Your daughter's no *child*. She's a full-blossomed woman under that unflattering dress. Scarcely her fault if a man or two who notices lacks couth and steps out of line.'

'Sir, do you presume to tell me my duty? Hezekiah, king of Judah, said the father to the children shall make known the truth.'

'Just friendly advice, is all. Seems to me your Bible learning needs a lick of tolerance to go along with it.'

'I commend to you Proverbs, chapter nineteen, verse twenty-nine, sir. "Judgments are prepared for scorners, and stripes for the back of fools".'

Elliot turned to Felicity. 'Now come, girl, we must be resolute in our faith and humble before God. Mr Dillard is partly right. The Devil has endowed you with the flesh of temptation. It's time to sweeten yourself with prayer and save yourself from eternal hellfire. Down on your knees!'

To Joshua's astonishment, Felicity knelt before her pa and he placed his left hand on her head and took the Bible from his wife with his right and raised it in the air.

Lifting his head, he intoned, 'Oh God the Almighty Father, look upon this Thy creature with mercy. Lead her away from corruption and into the path of salvation. Let her not be a scarlet woman. Give her the horse-sense to be Thy handmaiden, oh Lord. Amen!'

'Amen!' Felicity and her stepmother chorused dutifully.

'Rise, girl!' And as Felicity obeyed, Elliot added, 'But you are still to be punished for your shamelessness in inviting Mr Dillard to ride the buckboard beside you. You are forbidden to leave the house and yard for one month.'

'Oh, Pa! You know I like to visit Mrs Phillips. There's no call–'

'Silence!' Elliot snapped. 'I fear the company of Doctor and Mrs Phillips is leading you into ungodly paths, regardless of today's sin. Their Englishness, their science and their petty luxuries are abominations.'

'That's a lie!'

Joshua felt uncomfortable, but was fascinated by the growing spat.

Elliot cried, 'How dare you dishonour your parent! You've a sore need for guidance, and guidance you'll get. Go to the barn and await me there. And be on your knees again, girl!'

'Haven't we prayed enough?' Felicity asked, making for the door.

'The Book says, "And the daughter of any priest, if she profane herself by playing the whore, she profaneth her father; she shall be burnt with fire". Consider yourself let off lightly.'

Mrs Elliot showed Joshua to his quarters over by the stream. No one could sing the praises of this little log cabin made of earth and wood. Comprising a single room, one wall had collapsed and was roughly propped up. The windows were holes with wooden shutters. The mud-plaster roof was sagging. The sum total of furniture was a bunk plus a straw-filled mattress.

A smell of rot and old sweat hung in the close air.

'We can bring in more comforts from the house, should it be needful.' Mrs Elliot's tone implied it should not.

Joshua wondered whether it mightn't be wiser for him to move on. But where would he go? The town of Fort Harper was not an option given the state of his purse. Nor was

Greeley and its bugs, which Felicity had told him were absent here due to the cold nights.

And he thought it best for him to lie low in remoter parts till any excitement over the killing of the vice lord Victor Porteous in San Francisco had abated and been forgotten. Why should he make a possible manhunt, official or unofficial, any the easier?

Moreover, he didn't think he, or this wild country, had heard the last of Leigh Jordan. Not being on hand to witness how her inexplicable deal with the crooked Walt Sloane panned out would go against what was left of his Pinkerton detective grain.

Suddenly, a female cry of anguish, followed by a low moan, reached the dim and musty interior of the shack. Joshua was startled, but Mrs Elliot's face showed not a flicker of reaction.

Joshua looked out toward the barn, but could see nothing. The doors were closed and the structure baked innocently in the sun.

'Was that your stepdaughter, Mrs Elliot?'

She answered deadpan. 'Could be. She's an ornery filly. Always was, long afore she had to make the choice 'tween being a woman of sin or a woman of God.'

A stifled gasp, another moan ... Joshua was appalled at the evidence of his ears.

'Is Carver Elliot thrashing her?'

'Something. Chastisement is good for the soul, Mr Dillard.'

'Seems a mite excessive,' Joshua muttered to himself in disbelief.

Mrs Elliot tightened her lips some more. 'God's will be done.'

'Carver Elliot's will, more like. Do you approve of oppression and abuse?'

That set the woman off.

'Questioning is wickedness! The Devil lies in ambush for the unwary. Does he not sneak into the very homes of the worthy, using the minors of the righteous to pervert them? The impudent flesh of a sassy temptress must be scourged fitly to destroy vanity and manifest the error of her ways.'

All this was delivered in the toneless whine of a long-time convert repeating a familiar catechism.

It also reinforced Joshua Dillard's decision. He generally made it a rule not to get involved in a family affair, but while a young woman was at the frightening mercy of such monsters, he'd stay around, waiting his chances to improve her lot.

So he pitched in over the following days,

chopping wood, hauling water, driving in the milk cows – anything these people asked or he thought it might take to win their confidence.

Carver Elliot, however, remained obdurate about Felicity's grounding, and it was this that upset the girl most, regardless of what had happened to her in the barn. In fact, she was at pains to avoid speaking of that part of her punishment, although it had left her tearfully distressed a full day.

This Joshua could understand. It would be tactless to question her. For a young woman at any time and in any place, whatever her father had done would be too painful, too awkward to mention, an ordeal she suppressed with her mind even while her heart ached.

But Felicity was truer to her given name than to her father's or stepmother's nature. Maybe she was just happy having someone she could talk to about inconsequential things.

She blushed when, clearing scrub behind the main house, he asked her about Doctor and Mrs Phillips. She'd brought him a tin mug of buttermilk which she set down on a stump before answering.

'They're my best friends. They live in a

beautiful little house in a bottom back toward Fort Harper. Melville' – she blushed again – 'that is, Doc Phillips is a very clever and kind man, a skilled physician from England who only came here for his wife's sake.'

'She had some attraction to Colorado?'

'No. Not really. She came for the "camp cure" but it hasn't worked and Mel – *Doctor* Phillips is real worried that Bess should be so sickly from the pulmonary disease. And folks hereabouts, like my pa and Mountain Hank, don't set no store by his medical knowledge, so he must try to farm, which he's very bad at – except for his rose gardens, of course, which the cruel folks call prissy.'

Joshua killed the smile her torrent of enthusiasm brought to his lips.

'So is Dr Phillips more of a gentleman here than a professional?'

'Oh, yes! And Bess is a real lady with culture and fine dresses, just the sort they wear in Paris and London and Edinburgh. I want her to teach me 'xactly how to be a lady, with refined manners and all. How to walk, how to talk, how to eat at a high-toned table... I want to learn *everything*.'

It sounded like Bess was a touchstone for all Felicity's aspirations. And Melville Phillips? She had a girlish crush on him, Joshua surmised. It seemed a crime she was prevented from going calling, was deprived of the only sympathetic ears she was likely to get.

Further probings revealed that Felicity often visited with the Phillips on her way into town on the buckboard to fetch supplies. This week, with Felicity confined to the property, that chore was to fall to Joshua.

'Your pa keeps pretty busy up at the sawmill most of the day,' he observed. 'I don't think he'd notice if you went missing a while. How say I take you to the Phillips on the sly? You could hide easy under the buckboard's tarpaulin. It ain't even folded, Just thrown in the back.'

'Oh, Joshua, do you think I'd dare?'

'Yeah. Why not? He'll never know, and you can tell your stepma you went picking flowers or somesuch in the woods. She ain't too smart, 'cept at parroting your pa's mean-spirited dogmas.'

'You're right. With you on my side, I don't need to put up with being cut off from my friends.'

Thus they laid what sounded like a safe and harmless plan, thinking it would work out fine.

7

DRUNK'S RAMPAGE

The Phillips's frame house sat in a fertile bottom among fields of hay, barley and squash.

But Felicity, having emerged hot and flushed from under the buckboard's tarpaulin, cast a critical eye and tutted as they approached. 'Looks like the grasshoppers have been chewing on their crops again.'

'Maybe the doc shouldn't try to make a living farming,' Joshua said.

Felicity leaped to his defence. 'But Dr Phillips has learned hisself how to milk his three cows. He has a coop with four fat laying hens and puts in his own crops. And aren't his roses just the prettiest sight you ever saw?'

Joshua admitted that the house and garden were a spectacle.

The house had a second storey and four rooms. On the east wall, its small side windows looked toward the just visible outskirts of Fort Harper.

The garden and its colourful roses – red, gold and white – were enclosed by a white picket fence. A painted shingle hung by chains from an iron bracket fixed to one of the gateposts. Neat signwriting said, 'Melville Phillips, M.D., late of London, England.'

Inside, Joshua found interior appointments quite luxurious for a frontier home – German bentwood chairs for one instance, a well-stocked, glass-fronted cabinet of Staffordshire pottery for another – although some things were beginning to take on a worn and faded look.

A glance across the titles on the well-filled bookshelves confirmed that the Phillipses were 'cultivated' people of learning and refinement. Volumes of English poets, like Keats and Tennyson, the historical romances of Scott and the novels of Austen were side by side with Darwin's *Origin of the Species* and Fyfe's *System of the Anatomy of the Human Body*.

Joshua could figure what Carver Elliot's response would be to this subversive display of erudition and liberality.

But under the polish the atmosphere was one of struggle and difficulty, too. Bess

Phillips was pale and frail; Melville Phillips, though personable, had the air of a man perpetually harassed and bewildered. Streaks of grey in his hair and furrows in his brow aged him, but Joshua suspected he was only thirty-some years old; his wife, about the same.

'You sure do have a green thumb, Dr Phillips,' Joshua said after he'd been introduced. He gestured toward a vase of cut roses that brightened the front parlour.

'Wish I could agree,' Phillips said. 'All the roses need here is plenty of watering. If only I could say the same about the damn' crops! Failures time and again...We're getting near the end of our tether, Mr Dillard.'

Bess Phillips, propped up in a rocker and wearing a shawl despite the heat, sighed weakly. 'Melville is a *doctor* really, you see. Give him a sick child for a patient and I swear he'll smile into its eyes and make it well. Roses are the same. Let him finger a rosebud and it bursts into bloom superbly.'

The effort of this and some more short speeches of no great importance left her nigh breathless.

Joshua resisted prolonging the polite discourse. The occasion was for Felicity; he had to get to town, call at the store, then return her to the Elliot place before she was missed.

Excusing himself, he was already out on the front porch when a smart buggy drawn by a pair of matching greys and carrying two persons swept up to the garden gate. The driver was lawyer Walt Sloane; the passenger, Joshua's erstwhile hirer and seducer, Leigh Jordan.

Sloane stowed the whip in the bracket and helped the New Yorker, still looking elegant in her new calf-skin vest and corduroy pants, down from the upholstered black-leather seat.

Joshua met them on the walk. 'Leigh! What are you doing here?' he asked.

'Well, I thought you would have remembered what my plans were, Mr Dillard. We're here to make a generous cash offer for Dr Phillips's piece of the valley. I understand from Mr Sloane that he should be more than ready to listen.'

Sloane, officious in a high beaver hat and tailed frockcoat, put an arm lightly round her waist and laid a restraining white hand on her sleeve. 'Say no more, Mrs Jordan. Tell him to mind his own goddamned business. Be reserved.'

'Now that's an unfriendly attitude, Sloane.

I'm sure Mrs Jordan has a mind and a voice of her own. A week ago she didn't need a man like you to do her thinking for her. Nor tell her how to conduct herself.'

Leigh clutched at the leather satchel she was carrying, and she wasn't nervous because of the barb in his last words.

'Possibly the confrontation with Mr Montgomery was enough for one day, Mr Sloane.'

Joshua's ears pricked up. So they'd come here after riding out to Mountain Hank's den at the far end of the valley, where the huge park finally gave way to mountainous terrain. He could imagine the kind of the reception Hank would have given them, and the bluntness of his answer to their overtures. Hank, an uncompromising holdover from an earlier era, had firm ideas about his solitude and the fastness of his rugged hideaway.

Sloane said, 'That man is a stupid drunk, Mrs Jordan. A relic and wreck. Doctor Phillips is a diff'rent case.'

Melville Phillips came out of his house. 'It's Mr Sloane from town, dear,' he called back to Bess. 'And a lady visitor with him.'

Nobody chose to correct the English medico's impression they were directly from town.

Sloane shoved past Joshua, seized Phillips's right hand and pumped it. 'Have I a deal to bring you today, Doc.'

Before much more was said, the situation, from being full of pretentiousness and insincerity, suddenly went to the ugly and frightening.

Joshua was going out the gate, heading for the buckboard, when noisy barking and the pounding of hoofs broke his step.

Mountain Hank, forking his big sorrel, lumbered into view. At a first glance, Joshua could see he was in a savage, bitter mood and drunk. He quickly guessed Sloane and Leigh hadn't so much left his property as been run off. Now he'd pursued them here to reopen the altercation.

Hornet, picking up on his mood like the one-man hound he was, circled the horse excitedly, giving tongue to angry snarls and yaps.

Hank wore an old pair of high boots, a baggy pair of tattered deer-hide trousers secured pirate-like by a frayed red scarf, and an unbuttoned leather shirt. His tawny hair and beard streamed in the wind, stringy after a week's neglect. His two pistols were stuck in the scarf and the top of his trousers and in his hand was a whiskey bottle.

He drew rein outside the Phillips's and drained the bottle, swaying in his saddle which was covered with a beaver-skin that had the paws still attached. Hornet came to a panting standstill, looking up at him with attentive, idolatrous affection.

Then Hank slung his empty bottle at the side of the buggy. It exploded, showering the roadway with broken glass and chips of shiny black paintwork.

'S-Sloane, yuh bastard! C'm 'ere an' face me like a man, will yuh? I'm gonna beat the snakiness outa your hide.'

But Walt Sloane had vanished smartly into the house along with Leigh Jordan and Doc Phillips.

Hank drew a gun and blazed it off twice in the air. Hornet began another round of barking.

Joshua yelled, 'Hey, quit that, Hank! You got no call to go scaring innocent folks.'

Hank fixed him with his eye which burned like a red coal. 'Get outa there or pull iron, Joshua Dillard! You think I ain't got the belly to go up against the land-grabbers, you're dead wrong.'

'Gunsmoke and blood ain't the way to straighten 'em out, Hank.'

Hank gave a great laugh that turned into a

boozy belch. 'Already backin' down, ain't they? An' that soft sawbones needs showin' afore he sells out.'

He was out for blood and, like a big old timber wolf on the scent, he wasn't going to give up till he'd tasted it. Whooping stridently, he galloped his snorting horse right around the fence line, firing his gun repeatedly. Then he pointed it at an upstairs window and shot out the pane.

A frightened woman's scream came from the house.

Joshua ducked back into the porch. For sure this was one of Hank's famed 'ugly fits' – the ugliest maybe. In hoorawing the doc's house, the mountain man had gone way over the top.

'Hank, you crazy cuss! One last time – are you going to quit that, or do I have to drop you out of the saddle?'

Hank, having emptied his first gun, whipped out its twin.

With greased gunspeed that baffled the eye, Joshua had his Peacemaker in his fist, cocked and aimed. Its crash resounded in the covered porch. Joshua sought to disarm Hank, but the waving target of the pistol-filled fist was too difficult, given its owner's erratic movements. He cavorted his sorrel this way and that, and his dog leaped and barked around the horse's hoofs.

Hank guffawed and threw a shot into the porch, scarring a white-painted timber upright in a shower of splinters, one of which nicked Joshua's right ear.

All in an instant, Joshua rushed forward onto the walk and dropped to his right knee in a crouch. He supported his right fist and smoking Peacemaker on his raised left knee.

With his second shot, Joshua did as he'd threatened. His forearm braced across his body, and going for the larger target of the man's massive left thigh, he scored a hit.

Hank roared and his big mount reared, whinnying. He lost his one-handed control of the reins and dropped his second pistol simultaneously. With the muscles in his left leg gone to sudden jelly, he was unable to keep his seat and slid backwards out of the saddle into the dust. He landed with a heavy thud heard inside the house.

Felicity came running. 'Stop it, you mad fools! Someone will get killed.'

'I reckon it's stopped already, Felicity,' Joshua said. 'I had to pull my gun on him purely in defence, or someone was going to get carried away from here feet first.'

Felicity, white-faced, nodded her understanding. 'Hank was drunk and angry. Is he hurt bad?'

'If we can get him inside between us, Doc Phillips can take a look and let us know, 1 reckon.'

Tense moments passed before Hornet, bristling with anxiety, would let them touch his master. It was then Hank himself who finally quieted the dog with a word or two gritted out through pain-twisted lips.

It took a third's help – Doc Phillips's – to lug the semi-conscious, sagging weight of Mountain Hank to the white-covered table in the back room.

Phillips bent over the table and stripped the rank leather covering off his involuntary patient's upper leg. The mountain man was lying face down, arms dangling limply over the table sides. Joshua's bullet had gone through his muscle-corded flesh, missing the bone, Phillips opined.

'It's badly torn up, however, and he's losing blood.'

Joshua and Felicity watched as the doctor did things with long, thin fingers that, though lately coarsened by the ravages of farm work, still held the ingrained skills of London hospital training.

Phillips worked quickly and in silence, first probing, then producing needle and thread to close the wound. His habitual frown deepened whenever Hank emitted a low groan. He finished the job by swathing the punctured leg in dressings and bandages.

'Bess,' he called. 'We won't be able to haul the hulk upstairs and he isn't mobile. Bring down some sheets, will you, and we'll make him up a bed on the parlour sofa.'

Back in the parlour, Walt Sloane and Leigh Jordan waited impatiently. They had maps and legal forms spread on the table beside Leigh's satchel.

Leigh was recovering her equanimity. 'Still running around with the farm girl, I see, Joshua,' she said.

'I try to help the persecuted where I can is the whole truth of it.'

'Very commendable.' Her words were loaded sweetly with sarcasm.

'I am what I am, not what you want me to be.' Joshua gestured at the table. 'And you won't be needing that stuff today. The doc's got other things to tend to now.'

'That smelly old squatter?' Leigh said. 'He's hardly anybody's concern. You gave him what was coming to him, Joshua.'

'No, Leigh, I blame you and Sloane for his

plight. You got him riled up and I reckon you oughta accept the consequences. I suggest you pay the doc for Mountain Hank's care, and consider yourselves lucky you aren't the ones with holes in 'em.'

Sloane jumped to his feet indignantly, scoffing. 'What bullshit, Dillard! I suppose it's just the sort of reasoning to be expected from a cheap gunhawk!'

'And the play you're making here is just what I'd expect from a slimy shyster with a caterpillar on his lip!'

Joshua turned to leave, acutely aware that time was passing and he had to go to town before he could smuggle Felicity back home.

But Leigh didn't quite manage to suppress a giggle at his retort, which pushed the infuriated Sloane beyond the breaking point of his temper.

Without warning, he threw a punch at the back of Joshua's neck.

Joshua staggered but didn't fall. Recovering balance, he swiftly bunched his fists and, on the turn, swung at the lawyer's pasty face.

The punch clipped Sloane's jaw, jerking back his head and reeling him into the parlour table, which was tipped onto two legs.

The maps and papers and Leigh's satchel slid off.

The satchel spilled its contents – more papers, letters, a framed tintype, a pearl-handled derringer, powder and paint, a tortoiseshell comb and brush, and the thousand and one gewgaws a glamorous travelling lady toted about with her.

Joshua barely noted any of these things as he lunged after Sloane. He grabbed the lapels of his frockcoat in a bunch with his left hand and hauled him to his feet. He drew back his right fist for a blow that would settle the sneaky lawyer's hash for once and for all.

Felicity cried out, 'Oh, no, Joshua! The Phillips have suffered enough. Don't let their home get mussed up anymore.'

Joshua looked around him at the room's already rumpled gentility. Then, saying nothing but growling disgust, he abruptly released his grip on the trembling Sloane's coat. The man collapsed to the Axminster carpet like a lifeless heap of discarded clothes.

Felicity swiftly planted herself between the two men. Bess Phillips compounded the girl's plea for an end to the mayhem when she let out a breathy wail and fainted away, slumping into the rocker, still clutching the clean sheets she'd fetched from upstairs. Consternation reigned, but the fist-fight was nipped in the bud.

Trying to save his battered dignity and avoid Joshua's scornful eye, Sloane started to gather up the contents of Leigh's bag. When he reached for the small tintype, Leigh snatched the photographic picture from him and stuffed it quickly into the satchel. Joshua saw only that it was hand-coloured por-traiture of a smiling man and an infant. Oddly, but impossibly, it looked familiar.

The evidence that Leigh was not intimate enough with Walt Sloane to let him handle her personal possessions gave Joshua a certain satisfaction.

'The hell with it, Felicity,' Joshua said. 'I'm out of here. I'll be back to pick you up in a half-hour, I guess. I reckon Doc Phillips will've sent these vultures packing by then.'

He strode out without further ado, glad to put some space between himself and the odious Sloane. He hoped he'd taught the man his lesson.

Leigh said, 'We'd better leave, too, Mr Sloane. I can see we'd be wasting our breath here today. You've played our cards all wrong.'

Sloane, who was checking for loosened teeth with a bitten tongue, flushed angrily. 'All right, Mrs Jordan. We'll go on to Carver Elliot's place.' He turned to Felicity. 'Is Dillard boarding at your pa's, girl?'

She nodded dumbly.

Sloane rubbed his fleshy hands. 'Good. I can't see Elliot approving of gunfighting and fisticuffs. When we tell him about the fracas here, I'm damned sure he'll kick Joshua Dillard out pronto!'

Felicity's heart sank. Her pa would hear she was at the Phillips's. Her goose was also cooked, sure as shooting.

8

DRYGULCHED!

'I don't know that going back at all is a good idea, Felicity. Your pa's likely to be rough on you...'

A note of query was in Joshua's voice as the buckboard bumped and rattled its way back to Carver Elliot's homestead.

'It's my only home, Mr Dillard,' Felicity

said, twisting a piece of her grey skirt between nervous fingers. 'Pa's done his worst to me before, but I shan't speak of that. And you can't cry over spilt milk, can you?'

She tried, but failed, to give him her enchanting smile.

A little later, Joshua asked gruffly, 'Haven't you endured his – sermonizing long enough? You sure you'll be all right?'

Felicity nodded awkwardly. All the happiness of their journey out was drained from her. 'Prob'ly... Oh, look – here comes Mr Sloane's buggy.'

Sloane couldn't get past them fast enough, running the offside wheels of the buggy through long grass.

'You're going to get your comeuppance, Dillard!' he jeered.

'Alone,' Joshua mused, when he'd passed. 'I wonder where he left Leigh Jordan?'

'Could be she left him,' Felicity said. 'She seemed none too pleased about what happened at the Phillips's.'

Bitter answers were waiting for them in the still and clear grandeur of the isolated upland park.

Carver Elliot met the buckboard in his meanest mood. His gaunt face was dark as a thundercloud.

'Get thee gone from my house, Satan!' he shrilled, pointing at Joshua. 'And you, wicked hussy, we'll see locked in the root cellar till you're ready to relent and do the penance that reveals your hidden sin!'

As soon as Felicity got down from the buckboard, her hair was seized in a vicious grip by her loveless stepmother and she was marched off to the house. 'A fine thing it is that ye've no gratitude for your mortification,' the woman said.

'You don't have to be harsh on the girl, you sanctimonious bastards,' Joshua said. 'There've been no improprieties done, and I take the blame in full for her disobedience.'

Elliot stormed on with his diatribe. 'You are a faithless, blaspheming gunman and bring shame and uncleanliness to my household. I evict you. Your warbag is thrown out already. God's will be done!'

'Amen,' Joshua muttered under his breath. 'I've put up with more'n enough of your ravings. Too right I'm getting.'

He walked over to the shack to collect his belongings, which he saw were strewn outside in the dust, much as Elliot had said.

What Elliot hadn't told him was that his quarters had already been spruced up with the 'comforts' he'd been offered unmeaningfully by Mrs Elliot. And a new boarder was in residence.

'Leigh!' he exclaimed, though he was only partly surprised having noted her absence from Sloane's buggy. 'I didn't reckon you'd settle for a lodging this rough. You must be cultivating a liking for the wilderness. The nights are cold, you know, and there won't be anyone to warm your bed.'

'That's an unpleasant remark, Joshua Dillard,' Leigh Jordan said stiffly. 'The cabin suits me just fine. I can keep a closer eye on my interests from here, and that's the pure truth of it. I figure Mr Elliot will soon be favourably disposed to my offer for his holding.'

But Joshua smelled a rat. There had to be more to her odd abandonment of the conveniences of hotel and town living than she was telling. Being a thin-blooded city dweller, it was not just barbed comment that Leigh would feel the cold up here. Maybe Walt Sloane had something to do with her strange decision.

He thought swiftly and hard, but came up with no obvious answer to the mystery. Yet he did let it have some bearing on what he determined to do next.

He discounted a return to Fort Harper. It

still wasn't an option, financially or because of its greater proximity to routes from San Francisco. Nor was it really any better than Greeley, despite its freer views on liquor and morality. Joshua suspected it was run in large part by Walt Sloane, his vigilance-committee toadies and his loafer hardcases.

Therefore, he would remain in what he believed the Indians had called 'The Great Lone Land', making camp on the banks of the rushing clear stream that flowed into the dam above Carver Elliot's sawmill. That would provide him with water, while his gun and some emergency rations in his bag would stave off hunger a while. With deadfalls abundant in the wooded glades and on the pine-clad slopes, he'd have no problem with fires and warmth.

He meant to stay close to the Elliot place, where he guessed the next chapter in the affair might be played out.

Back in Fort Harper, and much disgruntled by the way his partnership with Leigh Harper was panning out, Walt Sloane was busy making enquiries. He shrewdly suspected there was more to Leigh's agenda than she was letting on.

In addition, he wanted to know more

about the gunfighter and mercenary Joshua Dillard. The sonofabitch had now whupped him or his cat's-paws twice.

Sloane sent discreet enquiries by telegraph to his brother in New York, who shared the family propensity for scheming and who worked for a legal firm in that city, and to a Pinkerton contact in Chicago.

In the event, his first leads came not over the singing wires and through a clicking brass instrument, but by word of mouth. One of his loafer spies told him a whiskey drummer passing through had said two men from San Francisco were asking around the bars in Cheyenne after a man who matched Dillard's description.

They were hardcase types seeking to wreak vengeance for a beating the man had given them in a parlour house, and for gunning down their boss, who'd owned the premises. No, the law wasn't involved. It was a private matter – a sort of debt among the wilder-living they would settle themselves.

Perfect, Sloane thought.

Dates for the San Francisco incident and Dillard's arrival in Fort Harper matched up. He got to work, following up the lead.

Accordingly, several days later, two cold-eyed Barbary Coast gents of muscular build, with lumpy faces and big fists, climbed Sloane's stairs beside the dry-goods store.

Up on the slopes west of the Elliot place, Joshua Dillard looked down from behind a massive pine trunk on its buildings and yard.

Two men had ridden in on horses he recognized as being among those for rent that he'd looked over at the livery in Fort Harper. Strangers these men then, but with a familiarity he couldn't quite place. Maybe it was their riding clothes – second-hand range gear which didn't sit comfortably on their wide shoulders.

Carver Elliot spoke with them. About what, he couldn't hear at this distance, but they sure didn't look like praying types. Elliot gestured dismissively towards the purple gloom of the canyons and the ragged grey rock of the mountains whose pinnacles pierced the blue sky.

'Yeah, there's a lot of wild country out here,' Joshua muttered, supplying the words he figured Elliot might be mouthing.

The men turned their horses and rode out of the yard and sight, past a clump of scarlet poison-oak six feet high and down the far side of the ridge beyond it, their hats bobbing from view. Joshua – stupidly, it transpired – gave them no more thought.

Shortly after dusk, as he sat before a small fire at his favoured campsite a few steps back from the stream's edge, the tin mug Joshua was lifting to his lips was torn violently from his hand. From the black nowhere that was a nearby stand of wind-breaking timber, sounded the vicious crack of a rifle.

The single shot was followed instantly by a volley of others, as more than one attacker levered and fired again. But Joshua was already rolling clear. His manoeuvre plunged him into the rocky stream-bed – a wet, cold and hard place to go but providing him with effective cover.

'Jesus!' he breathed. 'That was a mighty near call.'

He gained the impression from the haphazard shooting that these men were inexpert with rifles. The first shot, far from being a clever one to throw a scare into him, had probably been aimed at his head.

Crouching low, he scrambled up the stream, half in and half out the water, till he reached a vantage point where he could peer over the bordering grey boulders.

The failing light was on his side. The attackers must have assumed his plunge into the stream was the tumble of a dying man. Two riders boldly left the cover of the timber and came looking for his body, their horses clattering into the shallows, sending spray flying.

Finding no corpse in the near vicinity, the men started downstream, assuming it to have been carried away in the flow.

The sun was well down behind the ranges and deep shadows filled the stream's course, though it was not yet full dark. Feeling the chill of oncoming night distinctly in his wet clothes, Joshua slithered backwards till he reached some brush reaching down to the water's edge. He crawled into it, then rose and ghosted through the trees.

He knew this piece of country far better than the drygulchers, whom he thought he recognized as the pair with the rented horses from the Fort Harper livery. It began to dawn on him that the men had ridden into the park looking for him; that they were enemies from his past, of whom there were many... Possibly his recent past.

He wondered what Carver Elliot had told them and who had pointed them to Elliot's anyhow.

Well, he might not have a Winchester, but he had his Peacemaker.

He made a short cut through the timber, coming out alongside the shed that housed Elliot's primitive sawmill. Here he waited in ambush, gun weighting his fist, for the bushwhackers to appear from upstream.

The hunted had become a hunter.

9

DEADLY HIDE-AND-SEEK

Late that day, in Fort Harper, Walt Sloane received a reply to his telegraphed enquiries to his law-clerk brother in New York. It was long, though not a word was wasted, and it gave him cause for deep thought.

He leaned on the counter and shook the flimsy sheet of paper with the missive on it in front of the nose of the town's telegraph operator.

'Listen, Spinetti, you don't say a word about this to anyone, you understand?'

The ageing operator's lined face tried to take on a look of indignation beneath his visor. 'Sure. I never talk about none o' your business, Mr Sloane, sir,' he said shakily.

Most of the townsmen were either Sloane's toadies or, if they were down-and-outs, dependent on the crumbs he threw them for carrying out his chores. Spinetti fell somewhere between the two camps, but he knew what was best for him. Moreover, this message that Sloane was so all fired-up about was largely unintelligible to him. Most of the people referred to were given initials only, for example, while New York geography and gossip were closed books to him.

'I'm glad of that, Spinetti,' Sloane said, with a curt nod.

He spun on his heel and stalked out of the telegraph office. He was rereading his brother's information as he went, pondering his next moves.

Parts of the puzzle were beginning to fall into place as he studied on it. One thing he couldn't figure was how deep a part Joshua Dillard had to play.

Still, he reassured himself, Dillard could be dead by now.

It was full dark and from his hiding place behind Elliot's sawmill, Joshua watched his hunters emerge from the blackness that filled the stream's gorge. They were on foot, leading their horses, as they searched in vain for his body.

'I figure he must've been swept all the way down, Carl. The sonofabitch is prob'ly at the bottom of this pond,' one said. He made a sweeping gesture that took in the body of still water behind the crib dam. 'It's the only answer for it I can see.'

Joshua was gratified to note that his voice was edged with exasperation.

'Reckon we should make sure, just the same,' Carl replied. He picked up a dead stick from the cherry-fringed edge of the pond. 'I'll go out across the dam and have a poke around. Like yuh say, Nort, he's gotta be around here someplace. Hold my cayuse, will yuh?'

Carl sidled out onto the timber and rock dam, picking his way across and peering into the dark water.

Nort looped the horses' reins around one arm and fished out the makings to build a cigarette. But he never got to smoke it, or even strike the match.

Joshua catfooted from behind the sawmill to a pile of cut logs, and from there into the shadows at the pond's edge. With a last rush he was on Nort, tipping his hat forward and smacking him across the back of the head with the solid iron of the Peacemaker.

The tobacco sack and box of matches fell with Nort's hat to the rocky ground, making a rustle of noise. Joshua caught the unconscious man and lowered him soundlessly to the ground. But the reins slipped loose from Nort's arm, and one of the horses was alarmed at the activity and backed away, stamping and snorting.

'What gives back there, Nort?' Carl called, sounding a mite testy. 'Yuh all right?'

Joshua put his hand over his mouth and mumbled gruff cuss-words. 'Damned frisky bronc!'

Out on the dam Carl gave a dirty chuckle. 'Yuh never was one with the horseflesh, Nort. Mebbe yuh should sweet-talk 'em like they was flesh without the hair!'

'Aw, go to hell, Carl!' Joshua rasped, then cleared his throat and spat, hoping that would allay suspicion about the thick strangeness of his voice.

'Waal, he ain't here, *amigo*. I'm a-comin' back. This is a fine ol' mess. Supposin' he ain't dead?'

''Course he's dead,' Joshua said, more confident that practice was letting him copy the accent and pitch of Nort's voice.

'Then it ain't our lucky night. The syndicate chiefs in San Francisco expect us to bring back proof.'

The name San Francisco brought the facts of it to Joshua in a flash. Of course these men were familiar. He'd first seen them at the Russian Hill parlour house. He'd downed the pair of them with his fists just before he'd had to shoot dead their vice-lord boss, Victor Porteous.

Carl stepped back cautiously across the dam, a darker silhouette against the indigo of the sky. But it was more than his footing he was worrying about. Somehow, he'd gotten wind all was not right with Nort.

He dropped his stick and drew a handgun.

Soon as Joshua saw, he snapped, in his own voice, 'I've got the drop on you, Carl. Throw down your piece!'

'Like hell I will!' Carl yelled. And he ran forward, reinforcing his answer with his gun as he came. He fired repeatedly and wildly into the darkness of the cherry thicket where Joshua was crouched beside the unconscious Nort.

Squealing in fear, the horses charged off up the stream-bed and into the night.

Joshua fired back before realizing his

gunflash gave Carl a target where before he'd had little or none.

Carl placed two more shots so close that Joshua felt the wind of one of the slugs as it screamed past his ear. He scurried back into the brush. Carl crashed in after him with no attempt at stealth.

Joshua fired one more shot to deter his advance, then he was through to the other side of the thicket. Knowing the lie of the land like the back of his hand after several days' camping there, he slipped across a glade and flung himself behind the stump of one of the bigger pines felled by Carver Elliot. By keeping his head low, he was most part hidden.

His shoot-and-run tactic forced the bush-whacker to break cover. And Joshua had more than his ears to rely on to know where he went.

The moon suddenly showed, and though less than half full and waning, the dim light afforded him a fleeting glimpse of Carl as he dodged behind the trunk of a dead pine.

Joshua waited. He reckoned he had only one option to end this, and he'd possibly get only one chance at it.

Both men played possum, but neither fooled the other.

When Carl finally lost patience and peered out cautiously from behind his tree, trying to locate him, Joshua shot to kill. It hadn't been of his making that it came to this, but he had to kill to stay alive.

The bullet took Carl high in the chest. It was the end of the trail for him. His gun slipped from his fingers and thudded into the soft mulch at his feet. He hugged his dead tree, as if it could keep him from going down, give him new strength though its own sap had long ceased to flow.

At the last, as his life ran out of him, he snarled a final curse. 'You bastard, Dillard! You goddamned, mad, yellow-bellied bastard! I'll be waitin' for yuh in Hell!'

Then his hands lost their grip and he slithered down the tree to the ground, his face rasping on the rough bark.

Joshua stole back through the thicket to where he'd left Nort out to the world, but maybe now stirring and once more dangerous.

One of the horses had returned and stood with trailing reins nearby. Of the other there was no sign. Nort hadn't moved an inch.

When Joshua came up close, he saw why. And it was a bleak discovery. One of Carl's first wild shots had hit his pard in the head.

Blood made a glistening dark puddle on the moon-white rock.

'Goddamnit! There's nothing anyone can do for you, mister.' He shook his head regretfully. 'It's a night for dying and no mistake.'

Then, knowing all his chances to ask questions were gone, he went through the man's pockets. In the man's vest, his search produced a well-known clasp knife. It had the name 'Joshua Dillard' engraved on it in elegant, flowing script chosen by his lost wife.

Next morning in Fort Harper, Walt Sloane summoned up to his office Buck Borden, the trustiest and most intelligent of his gang of hardcases.

'I want you to ride out to Carver Elliot's place, urgent, Borden, and deliver him this letter.' Sloane tapped the letter several times with his index finger. 'See that he understands it's important – mighty important. It can't be put off, not even if today's his favourite saint's day.'

Borden slouched out and thumped down the stairs, but when he'd gotten halfway he stopped, and the thumps started coming up again.

Sloane put down his raised coffee cup.

'What is it, Borden?' he snapped, as the roughneck loomed back in the doorway. 'The instructions were plain and I said it was urgent.'

'Carver Elliot's just ridden into town, Mr Sloane, an' I figure he's comin' up to see yuh already, seein's he's tyin' up outside the dry-goods store.'

Sloane's smooth face for once didn't mask his thoughts, but he covered up his surprise swiftly. 'Excellent! Ask him to come up straight away.'

'Must've gotten some sorta divine tidin's, I guess,' Borden said drily.

Carver Elliot was in a foul mood. 'Mr Sloane, those two men from San Francisco you directed to my property are dead. There was infernal shooting behind my place last night, and today the good Lord's first light showed me their bodies.'

Sloane stiffened. 'But Dillard! What about Dillard?'

Elliot shrugged. 'Skulking in the hills like the hell-dog he is, I would think. I likewise believe it was he who shot your visiting executioners.'

'Let me emphasize they were no men of mine, Mr Elliot,' Sloane said. 'But I sympathized with their intentions, and Dillard is certainly a man who hires out his gun – a friendless, lone wolf whom we mustn't trust a moment.'

Elliot stared back impassively, his eyes boring into the lawyer. 'You talk right out, don't you, Mr Sloane? But why give me this warning? I have my God to watch over me and need no other protection.'

'The why ties in with what I aim to disclose to you, Mr Elliot. I could throw a fortune into your lap – enough to keep you in clover until the time comes for you to ascend to that great mansion in the sky. Now listen close...'

It seemed, as Sloane had guessed, that worldly wealth did hold as much interest for Carver Elliot as the next among his fellow men. After all, was he not God's tool – frugal, sober, hardworking – and was it not written that the meek should inherit the Earth? Duty demanded that he show no reluctance in claiming the inheritance.

As for temporal law, Elliot was satisfied with his (Sloane's) assurance that what was proposed would not only make him rich and powerful, but complied with all the statutes of the State of Colorado and the Union.

Sloane completed their palaver with a reiterated warning.

'Remember, you must be on your guard against Joshua Dillard. I don't figure how he fits into this, if he does anymore, but he was hired out to Leigh Jordan. Could be he's an assassin. Until we've finalized the paperwork, you must keep both of them away from Felicity at all costs. Else, all might be forfeit.'

'Don't worry, Sloane. The girl's locked in my root cellar for her sins. I guarantee that that is where she'll stay, except for prayer and worship at seven daily and twice on Sundays. God's will must be well done, and done forever!'

But Walt Sloane didn't trust in the infallibility proffered by Carver Elliot. After he'd left, he called in Buck Borden and his fellow ruffian, Chaz Clancey.

'Dillard could be as dead as the Frisco men Elliot says he blasted. Or maybe he's wounded, or lit a shuck. But we can't trust to guessing.'

Borden rubbed a bristly chin. 'Mebbeso he's ridden out. The liveryman says one o' them hosses he hired out came back to town with an empty saddle, but the other's missing. Dillard coulda turned hoss-thief and moved on down the line.'

Sloane gulped the last of his cooling coffee

and swirled it round his mouth thoughtfully.

'It's too risky to bet on, Borden. You and Clancey will ride out and keep an eye on Elliot's place. If Dillard goes near, there'll be a big bonus for the man who stops him.'

'You mean, shoot him down, boss?' Clancey asked.

'Yeah. Like a coyote. Kill the sonofabitch. I can square it real easy, specially if you bring him back to town face down over a livery saddle. He's a horse thief, ain't he?'

10

WILD RIDE

Leigh Jordan was beginning to regret her hasty decision to take over the Elliots' cabin for rent. True, she'd gotten Joshua Dillard evicted, but the prime reason for the move – to put her in close, unshared proximity to the girl Felicity – had failed miserably.

In a way, she'd been hoist with her own petard. By letting Carver Elliot know the girl had been out visiting with the Phillipses – when she shouldn't have been apparently

– she'd led to Felicity's incarceration in the root cellar.

Leigh's patience was being sorely tried. Conditions in the ramshackle cabin were primitive and despite the Elliots' supplementation of its 'comforts' – chiefly a chair, a supply of candles, a cracked mirror and a tin basin – a lack of proper bedding made the nights cold. Bits of dirt fell on her from the roof, dislodged by every stiff breeze. She hadn't realized before just how accustomed she'd grown in her recent past to softer living.

One night she was kept awake by a heavy breathing and a sound like sawing under the floor. Elliot told her it had been a skunk sharpening its long claws on the underside of the planks. If she'd retaliated in any way, the release of its malodorous scent would have made her cabin uninhabitable. He set a trap and, fortunately, she wasn't bothered again.

On the Saturday, Elliot said that next day, the Lord's day, she was welcome to join himself, his wife and daughter in worship. 'We're distant from the churches here, and their ordinances, but we lay work aside and praise Him in a temple made by His hands.'

He took in with a wave of his own the

natural surroundings. In the brilliant sunlight, they were indeed awe-inspiring – the solemn mountain peaks, the ages-old, dark-green forests, and the park's pastures brightened by dandelions, buttercups, violets and other wildflowers, blue and yellow, to which she couldn't put names.

Leigh had heard their daily worship in the mornings. They sang no hymns, which the strict Elliot regarded as irreverent, but he would chant some psalm or other to a funereal tune, they would read a chapter from the Scriptures, and say prayers which were as much a condemnation of godless fellow-men as a thanksgiving to their Master.

So she cried off. A Sunday service could be only more of the same and even less palatable. 'I think I'll go visiting poor, injured Mr Montgomery at Dr Phillips's, if I might borrow your buckboard,' she said.

She thought this sounded a sufficiently lofty occupation for the Sabbath. It might also afford the chance to follow up her land-buying proposals, which were, after all, her ostensible reason for being in the country.

To her surprise, Elliot appeared pleased at her decision and gladly granted her the use of the habitually docile mare Sally and the buckboard. Maybe it was because he didn't want her near his daughter, who'd be released for the special worship. Or was she being obsessive, suspecting that he might somehow have gotten some glimmering of her true motives here?

No, that was impossible.

Joshua Dillard was aware of the presence of the two hardcases patrolling the park in the vicinity of Carver Elliot's homestead long before they were aware of him.

He recognized Buck Borden and Chaz Clancey as members of Walt Sloane's bunch of losers ... the same two he'd had his previous run-ins with in Fort Harper.

It seemed likely the non-return to town of the San Franciscans had been noticed and Borden and Clancey had been despatched to check this out – maybe to kill him if they discovered the first pair had failed in the task.

Joshua now had his own mount, one of the livery horses, a roan, that had been ridden out here by either Nort or Carl, and which he'd rounded up. Not only was he mobile, the two ex-miners were no trackers, that was for sure. Anyway, if they had have been, Dillard knew enough tricks to keep the best

Indian sign-reader guessing.

He decided to let Borden and Clancey see him. It would be interesting to find out whether they'd give chase or stay roughly put on some kind of guard over Elliot's.

With the roan had come a Winchester rifle, of the model known as the Improved Henry, stowed in a saddle scabbard. The magazine had been reloaded since he'd been fired on and carried a full sixteen .44 rimfire cartridges. Mounted up and ready, Joshua rode from the cover of a patch of timber and used one shot to bring attention to himself.

Borden and Clancey, who were lounging on a grassy ridge in the sun, keeping a lacklustre eye on Elliot's yard and corrals, shouted at one another. Borden pointed.

Joshua wheeled the roan and set off at a canter. The hardcases ran for their horses, which stood with dropped reins, and swung into leather to race after him.

It was what Joshua had expected and he was going to give them a run for their money. He headed west at full gallop into the mixed terrain.

He'd fixed on making it a long ride through sloping pastures; deep, vast canyons, filled with purple shadow; ancient, blackish-green pine forests; along the shores of a still, blue lake; and over terraces and past upthrusts of rock, weather-stained and, though mostly granite grey, sometimes brilliantly coloured by ores – red, buff, orange and green.

He didn't need to look back. Distant shouts and the thunder of hoofs told him Borden and Clancey were riding hell-for-leather in pursuit.

Since he'd had the horse, Joshua had made many exploratory rides over the upland valley and the Rocky Mountains foothills. He was gratified when he quickly learned that he knew the lie of the land as well as, or better than, his pursuers. As he'd summed them up before, they were ex-miners, now townmen and loafers looking for an easy life. They weren't woodsmen, hunters, or even horsemen of any great ability. Probably their mounts were from the livery again, or loaned by some vigilance-committee toady of Walt Sloane.

Joshua grunted. 'Yeah...' he said softly. It all came back to the sneaky lawyer. Doubtless it was once more Sloane on whose orders they were acting.

One leg of the ride was a rugged ascent through a ravine threaded by a rapid, snow-born trout stream the stony bed of which also frequently served as their trail. Through an unexpected opening to the west, Joshua glimpsed the glistening outline of the Snowy Range – the backbone of the continent – winding through the wilderness of the ranges.

Circling somewhat, Joshua re-emerged in the upper reaches of the park. He then lost the chasers while cutting through a stand of pines, so he took out for Mountain Hank Montgomery's squatter's claim, looking for soft ground and being careful to leave plain tracks. He didn't want to punish the roan and at Hank's were the chances of rest, water and graze.

Hank's home was a rough, black log cabin with a mud roof. It looked more like a wild animal's lair than a man's dwelling, though the ill-fitting, warped door was padlocked. Hank, presumably, was still at the Phillips's, recuperating from his thigh wound.

The roof was covered with skins, mostly beaver, laid out to dry. The carcass of a deer hung at one end of the cabin attracting flies. The antlers of deer, old horseshoes and bits of rotting tackle were strewn about the unfenced yard.

Joshua slackened off the roan's saddle, but was careful not to let the animal drink to excess, lest it developed stomach cramps.

'I know you'd like more, but the job ain't done yet,' he told the horse.

The day was wearing on and the shadows lengthening when Joshua spotted Borden and Clancey skylined on a ridge, doggedly pounding along in his tracks. Their mounts' heads hung and Joshua imagined that at closer quarters he'd be able to see the lather and hear the breath whistling through their nostrils.

It was no way to treat good horseflesh, but Joshua grunted in grim approval.

He retightened the cinches on his rested roan but stayed put till they caught sight of him. Then he smiled to himself, stepped up into the saddle and loped the roan away. A bullet winged past him, but the distant rifleshot was plenty wide and its velocity about spent.

Putting Hank's den and some tall silver spruce, which had dense conic crowns of blue-green needles, between himself and his hunters, Joshua headed back into the shadowy canyon country. The grey and white-spotted roan would be especially hard to spot in such territory as darkness fell.

He found the place he wanted and rode upstream through foot-deep water for about a half-mile. Then he put the willing roan up the bank and climbed a steep defile in an overhanging wall of granite to a plateau. The route might once have been a bear track.

The top, when he reached it, was spread with great slabs of shelving rock, but there was considerable grass. And no recent sign of bears. He didn't think Borden or Clancey would figure to scramble up the defile, and the graze's distance and isolation from other ways of access made its more roundabout discovery unlikely.

It was at least a four-hour ride back to the Elliot place by the most direct route. The sun was setting in golden glory, but the canyon he'd left behind was already filled with gloom. He off-saddled his horse, removed the blanket and rubbed the beast down. Finally, he tethered the roan to a stout juniper.

'Were I you, hoss,' he said, 'I'd rest easy for a spell, but I've got new tricks to pull on these jaspers.'

If he read their oafish minds aright, Borden and Clancey figured they'd gotten him on the dodge and had the upper hand. They'd know that with darkness falling, he'd not be able to return to the Elliot place over the broken country through which he'd fled. Likely as not, they'd have grub and gear with them for the purpose of camping out and maintaining their original watch. Lured away from that, they'd now be apt to bivouac in the canyon and resume their manhunt in the morning.

He hurried back on foot to a vantage point which allowed him a view into the shadows of the canyon.

With only a rosy afterglow reaching the parts of its floor least obscured from the western sky, it was difficult to make much out. But Joshua pinpointed his enemies by the sound of their grumbling as they picketed their horses on a patch of grass beside the fast-slowing stream.

A little later they lit a fire. Dead brush and sticks crackled. The tempting aroma of strong coffee, bubbling as it boiled in blackened pot, reached Joshua's nose. By the firelight he could see them clearly.

Buck Borden stared impassively into the fire. Chaz Clancey slumped over his crossed legs, dozing.

Eventually, they bedded down for the night and Joshua moved into the next phase of his plan. By moonlight, he began a dangerous descent of the cliff face, along the rim a piece from the hardcases' camp.

It took him a full half-hour. Once, dislodged stones trickled down beneath him, bouncing and rattling so loudly to his ears that he feared Borden and Clancey would be alerted. But above the constant chuckle of the stream they heard nothing they thought to associate with him.

Joshua was glad to reach the stream bank in one piece and undetected. Maybe it would have been easier to have gone back to the defile he'd ascended on horseback and made his way down there. But time might be of the essence. How long would the pair sleep?

Joshua sneaked past their camp, Peacemaker drawn and eyes peeled for the slightest sign he'd been detected. But he'd worn them out, it seemed, and they were in a deep slumber.

He went on to where the two horses were standing. There, he pulled out the picketing pins, and waved his hat in the animals' faces, sending them backstepping. But they were too placid – or too tired – to be spooked and run off.

'Go, you stupid lumps, go!' he dared to whisper hoarsely.

They took some more steps, tossed their heads a bit, snorted, but didn't whinny, nor so much as roll their eyes. He couldn't figure whether they were dead-beat or plain ornery stubborn.

Joshua was depending on leaving his pursuers afoot when he rode out at first light. He aimed to ride the roan lickety-spit to Fort Harper – maybe going via the Elliot place – and find out what the hell was going on.

Walt Sloane figured largely in his vengeful thoughts. He was also beginning to feel a twinge of guilt about how he'd left Felicity Elliot to suffer her parents' wrath, despite his long-held belief that his line of business didn't include interference in family issues.

But if the damned horses couldn't be taken out of the equation, the journey back might not be possible without killing another two men first.

Or maybe they would kill him.

Joshua was starting to think about the San Francisco toughs he'd been forced to shoot above Carver Elliot's dam when a possible answer came to him in a flash.

11

FELICITY'S ESCAPE

Joshua scooted on further downstream, at first carefully watching where he put his feet. The crack of a snapping stick might be all it would take to jerk Borden and Clancey awake and squash what he had in mind for putting the horses to flight.

It was the thought of Elliot's crib dam of timber and rocks that had given him his idea.

Past the hardcases' camp and the patch of green where they'd tied their horses, he'd noticed the canyon narrowed and the stream was partially blocked by a boulder. Another was poised atop it, the result of the same slip that had tipped the first into the watercourse. If he could topple the second rock into the stream, too, he could quickly block the fast flow by piling more debris behind the obstruction … his own make-shift crib dam.

Before long, with the stream blocked, the

patch of grass where the horses were would be under water. A little later, the hardcases' campsite would be flooded as well.

If that didn't persuade the horses to clear out of there, nothing would. To boot, Borden and Clancey would be thrown into confusion in the darkness.

Joshua arrived at the narrows and looked around for what he needed to do the job. He found an almost straight tree branch – or maybe it was a sapling's trunk – splintered off in a storm at higher altitudes and washed down the stream till it had lodged against the big boulder. The timber was too hard for it to be pine, and it suited what Joshua had in mind perfectly.

He climbed up on the boulder and inserted the jagged, narrower end of the timber under the base of the smaller boulder. He heaved against it, using it as a pry-bar. He flung his weight into the task, straining muscles right through his body and breaking into a sweat. The boulder started to move but settled back as soon as he relaxed.

He grunted, took a deep breath and applied the leverage a second time.

It was on the third attempt that the boulder finally shifted for good, grating past the point of no return and rumbling down from where it was perched, smashing into the water with a mighty splash that fair soaked Joshua. Fortunately, the spot was too far from Borden and Clancey for the noise to wake them after their strenuous afternoon of riding.

Joshua scooped up handfuls of other debris that had collected at the scene and piled it behind the two boulders. The fast current packed it into the chinks. The water flow below the reinforced obstruction diminished rapidly, while the level behind it rose and rose.

Joshua quit the place, hauling himself up the steep canyon face. Handholds and footholds weren't too hard to find, but each one had to be tested before he could trust it with his weight.

'Be stupid to take a death dive after such a stroke of genius, and that's the pure truth of it,' he muttered to himself.

Felicity Elliot, confined to the root cellar, wondered how much longer she could endure Carver Elliot's persecution – in particular, the demands she named even in her own thoughts only as his 'pestering'.

She knew it wasn't right that a father should treat a daughter so, but her pa was a

God-fearing man, wasn't he? He read his Bible and he prayed long and hard every day. He knew all the Higher Laws that were set above those of mankind – and above the quibbles of ignorant womankind, like her sinning and miserable self.

She could look for no help from her step-mother, who was equally vile and relished her degradation. She believed, too, that her stepmother benefited from it in a more prac-tical way. A drudge herself, she protected jealously the relief it gave her from like attentions.

Felicity lost count of the passing days in her misery and the constant gloom of the root cellar, but she knew that Sunday would soon be around when she'd be allowed up not just for morning prayers, but for the lengthy rigmarole which for her pa con-stituted Holy Worship on the Sabbath. That, she made up her mind, was when she'd make a break for freedom.

She'd make a run for Dr Phillips's house, confess her sad story, of which Bess alone momentarily knew the smallest part, and ask for their help.

She knew the flight on foot might take all day – maybe longer if Carver Elliot came after her and she was obliged to dodge and hide. Also, that Melville Phillips, although very pleasing in his manners and appearance, was not a forceful man, and that Bess was a very sick woman.

But what other course of action was open to her? Maybe Melville could loan her money, although he had little to spare. With money she could buy a ticket for Denver. There, she was sure a young woman like herself, already forcefully stripped of her scruples, could find paying work.

Felicity surveyed her prison. It contained no obvious aids to escape.

The cellar's floor was hard-packed dirt. A large stone mass supported the structure of the chimney stack above. The one high window had a grille with six vertical bars on the outside and a wooden shutter on the inside. The shutter would open only enough for ventilation, and the room was kept in almost complete darkness.

Part of Carver Elliot's creed was a frugal 'waste not, want not'. But putting it into operation was a duty that invariably fell to her stepmother and herself. Shelves were packed with stored root vegetables – potatoes, carrots, turnips, beets, onions – and certain fruits, like apples. The place was dry, had an even, low temperature, yet afforded protection from the severe Colorado frosts that took winter night-time temperatures many degrees below freezing point.

Eggs, which the chickens laid when there was plenty of daylight, as in summer, were put away every fall. They were pickled in crocks, with salt, water and unslaked lime, to make them last 'almost to the crack of doom' according to her stepmother. Many of the vegetables were also pickled.

It was a pickle crock that Felicity hit upon as the means to salvation from her cruelly religious home. The crock was an ovoid brown vessel of good size and weight. She'd make use of both the hefty stoneware and the contents.

She unstoppered the crock in readiness and placed it in the darkest corner beside the rudely cut steps that led up to the cellar door.

She also began to pay more attention to the routine of the household above her. An absence of noise from chores at last confirmed her belief that Sunday had dawned. When Mrs Elliot came to fetch her for the farcical ritual of the isolated family's morning service, she was ready – tense with nervousness and impenitent excitement.

'Felicity!' Mrs Elliot whined from the

open doorway at the top of the steps. 'Bring your worthless self up.'

'Coming, Ma,' Felicity said, her voice wobbling. She dipped at the foot of the steps and hoisted the crock, holding it close behind her, hiding it as best she could with her skirt.

'Get a move on, girl,' the woman urged, her eyes not yet adjusted to the cellar's darkness. She wrinkled her nose in a sniff of disapproval and put a sneer in her twang. 'It's time to call on the Lord for forgiveness, and to learn the ways back from your downward path.'

When Felicity reached the top of the steps she dashed the crock's brine full in her stepmother's face.

The strong liquid stung Mrs Elliot's eyes, but the cry she uttered was cut off. The full force of the swung crock struck her in the back of the head and sent her toppling down the steps to the cellar floor. She landed on the dirt in a moaning heap.

Felicity didn't stop to study on the results of her violence. Her pa sat reading his Bible at the bare table in the parlour. She dashed through.

He started to his feet. 'What in God's name...? Stop, girl!'

Felicity was still toting the pickle crock. She threw it at him with all the force she could muster. It hit his long legs, bringing him down as he rose, then careered into a table leg where it broke into two large pieces and several shards. Eggs, incongruously visceral and corpse-white, rolled on the plank floor.

But all this Felicity barely noticed. She fumbled open the door latch. She rushed out into the yard, slamming the door shut behind her.

Emerging from the pines and coming across the rolling green meadow, on horse-back, she saw Joshua Dillard.

She ran toward him, sudden hope in her eyes.

Joshua Dillard cursed himself for all kinds of a fool. They should have called him Joshua Hard-luck, he thought with a wry grimace. Hard luck always seemed to turn up in his life just when he least needed it.

The damming of the river had sort of worked, but only as a half measure. Half success? Half failure? That he couldn't make up his mind about, yet.

Borden and Clancey's horses had moved off sure enough when the water flooded their patch of graze. The men had awoke in a fury when a widening pond lapped at their feet.

They leaped up, grabbing the saddles on which they'd rested their heads, and went almost immediately to where the horses had been picketed. Finding them gone, they filled the darkness with profane cusses that echoed up and down the canyon, causing more disturbance than the distant, mournful howl of mountain wolves.

Joshua stayed around no longer. It was impossible to see what went on in the dark down there, anyway. Leaving the canyon rim, he went back across the frosted grass to where he'd left his roan. As soon as the blacks and deep greys of the canyon country turned to purple and the eastern sky took on a rose-red flush, he saddled up and began the ride back to the Elliots'.

He rode at a leisurely pace, an easy lope, till, topping out on a ridge, he glanced back. The lemon-coloured sun had quickly enlarged into a dazzling globe which illuminated his backtrail. And it filled him with despondency to see two riders flogging along a single horse relentlessly in his tracks.

Only one of Borden's and Clancey's docile horses had apparently wandered far enough to elude the two toughs. They'd rounded up the other and now, mounted double, they were set on running the once decent-looking bay gelding into the ground, maybe to its death, to catch him.

Feeling a stab of pity for the animal, Joshua wheeled his own, flicked the reins and resumed his ride at a gallop. He out-paced Borden and Clancey without distressing his roan and they were soon lost from his sight.

Hard luck always managed to seek him out, Joshua reflected. It clung to him like his own shadow, dogged him every step of the way. This time he'd asked for it. He should have known better than to stay in the wild country. It had done himself and every other deserving being no good at all.

In this adventure, the mishaps had started before he'd met his client, with the unpleasantness in San Francisco. Going to Fort Harper instead of staying in Greeley had been a mistake, too. He'd run foul of the smart and odious Walt Sloane, and had upset the woman who'd hired him, rich and beautiful Leigh Jordan. Just when he'd thought he'd righted the last, he'd discovered that sharing her bed had only added to his woes. Going to the aid of Felicity Elliot, an innocent damsel in distress, had cost him Leigh's patronage.

He shook his head sadly on remembering that. He never would figure out how the female mind worked. Could jealousy really have such a strong effect?

Helping Felicity had, in the long run, done her no favours either. Smuggling the dear girl to the Phillips's house to visit with her only friends had worsened her sad domestic plight and brought her more abuse. Carver Elliot's methods for drawing a lost sheep back to the foot of the cross were disturbingly irregular.

No, this time he'd done nothing right! And once again, his various interventions left his pockets empty.

Deep in black thoughts, Joshua rode the trail through a dense and ancient forest, silent except for the eerie sigh of the wind through the pine needles and the muffled clop of his horse's hoofs.

He'd be damned if he'd let Borden and Clancey think they'd put him to ignominious flight.

Before he rode out of Colorado altogether, he'd ride by Carver Elliot's place, put up the horse in the barn, and have more words with the pious fraud and his downtrodden wife in a last bid to take responsibility for Felicity's 'sins' and improve her lot. Maybe he'd also see how his erstwhile client was making out in her primitive cabin. Leigh Jordan roughing it might be good for an inner laugh – he sure could do with one.

Then, in a final pass through Fort Harper, he'd return the livery's 'stray' roan and confront Walt Sloane over the inept attempts on his life by Borden and Clancey.

It came as a complete surprise when he rode out from among the trees that crested the last rise before the Elliot homestead and was faced with the sight of Felicity running pell-mell across the yard.

'Joshua Dillard!' she cried. 'Help me!'

The door of the main house burst open and Carver Elliot himself came out, roaring with wrath, and set after the girl in hot pursuit.

12

'YOU RUN TO YOUR DEATH!'

Joshua kicked at his horse with his heels. He rode the roan helter-skelter down the slope.

Swinging the horse around so that he was heading in the same direction as Felicity, he rapped, 'Mount up behind, Felicity!'

He slowed the horse and kicked his left foot out of the stirrup. Felicity bunched up her skirt around her thighs, put her own left foot into the stirrup and, with a helpful heave from Joshua, swung her bare right leg over the horse's back.

'Aboard!' Joshua yelled. 'Now hang on tight!'

Elliot was running after them, taking great strides, but he was too late. His gaunt face contorted with anger and frustration.

'Harlot!' he spat after them, professing shock at the view of her sturdy legs. 'Cover your wicked flesh!'

'Oh, the foul hypocrite!' Felicity gasped, anguished and breathless. 'My legs are in no wise a secret to him.'

'You've gotta leave the sonofabitch for good, Felicity,' Joshua said. 'No life can be worse than the one you're living.'

Carver Elliot was left behind, shaking his fists to the heavens in frustration. 'You godless child! I fear you run to your death!'

But a new threat was on their heels. Joshua's detour to the Elliots' yard and the ride back onto the rough trail to Fort Harper had allowed Borden and Clancey to catch up on him. With his own horse now carrying a double burden, too, he'd lost the advantage he'd had over them. He couldn't draw away this time, even though the roan was still in better shape.

A shot was fired at them. Felicity felt its wind as it passed her leg and cried out.

'Goddamn!' Joshua snarled. He pulled the over-laden roan from right to left in a haphazard, jinking manoeuvre designed to dodge further lead. 'Where were you running, Felicity?'

'I was going to the Phillips,' she said, the words coming out jerkily as they thumped along. 'They might help me get to Denver.'

'Just now, with the Phillipses sounds as good a place as any to me. We aren't going to get much further like this.'

When they drew near the neat frame house, surrounded by its white picket fence, Joshua said, 'Isn't that your pa's little buckboard, Felicity?'

She was clinging close to his broad back, her arms round his waist, and had to peer round him to see.

'Why, yes. Maybe Leigh Jordan has borrowed it to come see Bess and Melville again.'

'Well, the more folks here, the safer you'll be, I reckon,'Joshua said. 'I expect Mrs Jordan is trying to buy their property. Jump down and run in pronto – soon as I pull up.'

Borden or Clancey took another shot at them from the rear, and Joshua's spine crawled. He wasn't comfortable bringing another exchange of gunfire to the Phillips's peaceful home but there was no help for it.

He brought the roan to a sharp standstill with a tug of the reins. Felicity spilled off its back into a heap in the dust, but she quickly regained her feet, gathered up her skirt and ran through the open gate and up the walk.

Sally, the Elliots' mare, scraped at the ground, shook her head and waved her tail like a whip at the sudden commotion. The buckboard to which she was hitched aft lurched as its wheels made a backwards quarter turn. The fence to which she was inexpertly tied creaked.

With Sloane's hired thugs riding up, doubtless intent on firing their guns some more, Joshua could see the reputedly calm Sally tearing the fence posts out of the ground and repeating the runaway performance she'd given in Fort Harper.

Meanwhile, the roan had reached the end of any reasonable expectation of its endurance. Prolonging the chase was going to wind it totally. And the plodding horse used by his pursuers had to be in a worse state. Joshua could see no sense in killing the animals. He resolved to make his stand here.

He drew the rifle from the scabbard, slipped from the saddle, and hit the roan on the rump with his open palm, sending it on its way unburdened. It uttered a whinny at the slap, or maybe from relief.

Joshua ducked behind the buckboard, where he drew out and opened his clasp knife. With quick slashes, he cut the mare's traces. It was a long time since mean Carver Elliot had spent money on harness. The leather strap was part-rotten on the far side, and Sally, increasingly disturbed, jerked free and trotted off toward Fort Harper in the wake of the disappearing roan.

Now Joshua had no means of retreat. He was committed to facing down his pursuers.

They came lumbering up on their ruined mount, a ridiculous spectacle except for the guns clenched in their fists. Boldly, Joshua rose up from behind the buckboard. He sent a rifleshot over their heads and operated the lever in readiness for a second.

The Improved Henry was an impressive piece of weaponry. Joshua knew it could fire its whole sixteen shots nearly as fast as a man could count without heating the barrel or failing to eject a cartridge shell. He hoped the two ex-miners knew what he was using and had a similar knowledge of its capabilities.

'This here Henry's near fully loaded,' Joshua called to them, as their unfortunate horse came to a side-heaving, sweating stop. 'You might want to try your luck, then again you might not.'

Borden laughed. 'There's two of us, Dillard. Yuh're a hoss-thief an' a dead man this time!'

'I don't think so, mister. Ain't rightly certain what it is makes you boys Sloane's puppets. His dirty money...?'

No answer came.

'Or maybe he makes you feel important.

Well, that's what I figure. You go tell him this – I'll be coming after him. Now throw your hoglegs down easy, and git!'

Clancey fired; Joshua fired. Clancey's shot spanged off a piece of ironwork somewhere on the buckboard. Joshua's ripped through Clancey's hatbrim, lifting the hat off his head. Then the two hardcases peeled off the teetering horse and vanished into the brush that bordered the opposite side of the road.

Joshua used the brief respite this gave him to turn his back on the buckboard, put his hands behind him under its nearside, and bend his knees. Taking a deep breath, he heaved with all his might. He grunted from the exertion. Muscles tightened to the point where he thought they'd tear. Veins knotted and throbbed as he tried to straighten up. He thought he might black out.

He'd lifted this damn thing back onto its wheels before, but that had been with the help of huge Mountain Hank. This time he wanted to tip it over onto its side, and he was alone.

It was no mean feat, but finally, in slow motion, the near wheels lifted off the ground and he was rising, straightening up. Then the weight left his aching shoulders. For a moment, the buckboard hovered at a point of no return before gravity came into play and it went down with a splintering, dust-raising crash.

Joshua's breath went out with a rush. It was done, and he was concealed from Borden and Clancey by the toppled conveyance's vertical tray.

Moments later, a fusillade of slugs from across the road drilled through the flimsy lumber, filling it with holes like the top of a big pepperpot. Several stray bullets buried themselves in the cladding of the Phillips's house.

'Nobody could live through that!' Borden said.

Nine eyes turned on Felicity when she burst into the doctor's parlour, breathless and dishevelled.

Mountain Hank Montgomery's was wild and dilated. He was reclining on the sofa – hot, dry and thirsty. He was still crippled by his gunshot wound and, though initially accepting of his plight, he was growing more despondent and confused by the day.

He wasn't a man to be cooped up indoors or fussed over. But Melville Phillips had delivered the dire diagnosis that his wound had become infected due to dirt on his clothing, of which pieces had been propelled deep into the puncture. It was an unassailable fact that, prostrated and restless, Hank found himself wanting in the energy to resist the warmth and rest the doc insisted he should have. He'd also been dosed with belladonna.

His wound was fierce and swollen. Red streaks radiated from the site and it continued to exude pus.

Bess Phillips's eyes were full of shock and fear. She'd heard the shooting, first at a distance, then drawing closer to the house. Moreover, she'd already been worried by the implications of the entreaties being made to her husband by the New York lady, Leigh Jordan. Should they really sell up their home? It was all too much for one so sick and poorly...

Melville Phillips's look overlaid perpetual harassment with astonishment. He never knew quite what to make of Felicity Elliot, but he found her a genuine person – quite charming in her unaffected ways and her enthusiasm for the 'refinement' denied her by an overbearing father. Deeply caring, he sensed dark shadows in her life that he'd like to lift. Yet she rendered him inexplicably tongue-tied, too.

Leigh Jordan's eyes turned cold as ice. Felicity had been hidden from her sight in the root cellar during all the time she'd been a boarder at the Elliot place. Now she had access to her – but how could she use it with so many looking on?

Hank's dog Hornet, sitting by the fire of pine logs kept burning constantly in the grate, turned his intelligent gaze on Felicity. He recognized her as a person who had his master's approval, and thumped his tail on the Axminster carpet.

'Felicity! Where've you been all this time?' Mountain Hank slurred.

Felicity realized he was close to delirium. She was distressed. She'd never expected to see the big, powerful man laid so low.

Bess gave a small cry and tried to raise up from her rocker, but fell back, the effort seeming to prove overmuch for her frail, wasted body. Her condition had deteriorated markedly in the week since Felicity had last seen her.

'Oh, you poor thing!' Bess said, unaware of how incongruous it was for her to be the one expressing concern. 'What is going on out there this time? Who are you running from?'

Melville Phillips jumped to his feet. 'My

dear girl, is the shooting something to do with you?'

Perceptively, Leigh Jordan said, 'Joshua Dillard's part of the ruckus, eh? He's bad company for you, Felicity Elliot. I'd advise you to shun him – from this moment on!'

Felicity answered none of the torrent of questions. She'd not recovered her breath before a bullet crashed through the parlour window, showering the room with vicious splinters of glass.

Hornet sprang up and began barking furiously.

Phillips, indignation overcoming caution, rapped out an oath – strong for him but mild by most standards – and strode to the window. Only by good fortune did he escape death as two more bullets whined into the room and others embedded themselves in the outside walls.

His wife lost all that remained of her colour and swooned, letting out a long sigh that no one heard.

Felicity began screaming incoherent warnings before she could stop herself.

Leigh Jordan dipped a hand into her satchel, and pulled it out clenched around the pearl grips of the derringer she carried there. Unexpectedly, the chance she'd been waiting for had been thrown into her lap.

Who would notice the sharp crack of one more shot, or that this one had come from within the room? Her thumb confidently cocked back the knurled hammer.

In all the noise and confusion, only Mountain Hank saw her point the small pistol at Felicity's back as the girl, still crying out, went to tug Melville Phillips back from the window.

13

A FIRE AND A SHOOTOUT

Mountain Hank let loose a rasping croak of warning.

'*Felic'ty ... g-uh-un!*'

It was such a strange and alarming sound that Felicity, having pulled Doc Phillips back from the window into the cover of the wall, turned quickly to see what was ailing him.

She'd already noticed Hank was in a feverish condition. His skin was flushed and he looked hot and dry. Probably the throat that could make a sound like she'd just heard was burning unbearably. Her first thought was that Hank was having difficulty breathing and was calling for her help. Her second was that restlessness was a trait that typified the mountain man at the best of times, while mania was common enough when he'd been 'on a spree'.

But this strange cry was something different from the symptoms of his delirium. As she immediately saw on turning, Hank wasn't the victim of some ghastly hallucination.

Leigh Jordan had a tiny, twin-barrelled pistol clenched in both hands. It was pointing directly at her, and Leigh's finger was wrapped around the trigger, whitening as it tightened.

Felicity was frozen with astonishment.

Mountain Hank, unable to rise on his wounded leg, flung himself bodily – and he was a big body – off the sofa. He crashed into table, chair and Leigh Jordan all at the same time and sent the three flying. He wrapped his massive arms round Leigh's legs and held them tight.

But the woman kept her grip on the derringer unbroken, her face a twisted mask of fury.

Hornet, who'd been cowering behind

Hank's sofa, leaped into the fray. Where Hank went, he followed. He didn't need orders. He knew all his master's enemies. In fact, the only order he might ever have needed was one to call him off. He was that kind of dog.

His great jaws closed on Leigh's right wrist. She shrieked. The gun wavered – and then it went off.

The large-bore slug whistled across the crowded parlour, missing everyone but shattering an oil lamp standing on the carved mahogany mantelshelf. The lamp's contents spilled into the fireplace and onto the glowing pine logs.

Whoosh!

The room was lit up by a flash of flame. Tongues of fire escaped the grate and migrated rapidly across the Axminster carpet, consuming papers that had fluttered from the smashed table.

Melville Phillips seized up a small shovel that companioned the poker by the fireplace and beat at the flames. 'Water!' he cried. 'Fetch water!'

Felicity ran to the kitchen and took up a bucket which she filled at the pump. But when she returned to the parlour, she was stunned.

In the dry atmosphere, flames had climbed rapidly up fabric chair covers and window curtains. They were licking at the legs of the bentwood furniture. The shelves of books were beginning to smoulder; glass in the china cabinet exploded in the growing heat. Everywhere, choking smoke swirled.

Bess, she saw through the black clouds, was passed out in her rocker. She threw her puny bucket of water in that direction, but the roaring flames were unquenchable.

Through the blinding smoke she saw Melville Phillips grab Mountain Hank under his armpits and try to drag him off Leigh Jordan who was trapped under him. Though Hank had seemingly lost consciousness, his grip around the woman was vice-like and their combined weight was too much for the doc. Flames plucked at the pair's hair and clothes.

Coughing, Phillips beat at the flames frantically with his bare hands.

The instant the buckboard had landed on its side, Joshua began backing away in a crouch. The band of his flat-crowned hat was stuck to his forehead with sweat. He went through the garden gate, and up the walk, keeping the obstacle between himself and the road, where Sloane's men hid in the brush opposite, guns at the ready.

As he expected, the overturned buckboard took a thorough drubbing from their lead. The bullets tore through the planks and bounced, spent, all about the Phillips' rose garden. A few missed the buckboard and hit the house; glass crashed. But their target absorbed the greatest part of their fire.

He heard Borden say, 'Nobody could live through that!'

Joshua chuckled to himself. 'Atlas has left that there theatre, fellers. A few more moments is all, and the sky's gonna fall in on you.'

Shoulders still aching from his exertions, he reached the porch, from where he crawled quickly round to the back of the house.

Beyond a tidily built chicken run was a rutted paddock where Hank's big horse grazed on scanty grass that appeared to be affected by a blight which Phillips, with his limited knowledge of ranching, had been unable to control. Patches of grey, wind-blown dirt were taking over. The forlorn sorrel stopped cropping the yellowed stems and looked at him slanchwise, full of hopeful curiosity.

To the right, the slope undulated. Scrub fringed taller vegetation such as cotton-woods and aspens. With the house now between himself and his attackers, Joshua made across the paddock for the trees, using the foliage there as cover and toting the Improved Henry.

West of the house, the wild growth reached right down to the road and Joshua was able to double back out of sight toward where Borden and Clancey stood boldly on the open right-of-way, brandishing their handguns in the direction of the spilled buckboard.

A flock of birds rose on whirring wings from the branches above Joshua's head. Sloane's two hell-raisers were too eaten up with their own imagined success to take notice.

'C'mon outa thar, Dillard, if'n yuh gotten life yet to crawl,' Clancey jeered.

'Aw, he's dead fer certain, Chaz,' Borden said, shoving his gun back into his belt. 'Let's haul out his stinkin' carcass an' take it inta Fort Harper.'

Joshua put the rifle to his shoulder and fired a single, well-placed shot that ripped off the heel of Clancey's boot, pitching him into the dirt with a startled curse.

Joshua placed the rifle on the ground and kept walking toward the two hardcases, who watched his advance, mouths agape and jaws sagging. His right hand was hovering over his holstered Peacemaker.

'I ain't dead yet, you ornery bastards,' he growled. 'But either of you still want the chance to change it, I'm about set to accommodate you.'

'He's broke m'foot, Buck,' Clancey moaned. 'The sonofabitch had yuh fooled.'

Borden recognized that the chips were down. Dillard was challenging him, prodding him like he'd prodded so many others himself – a bully by nature and the tool of Walt Sloane by lazy choice.

'Mebbe so, Chaz. But I tell yuh – it's the last stunt he's gonna pull.'

'I'm ready soon as you want, Borden,' Joshua said. 'Let's finish this business.'

Borden's hand dipped for his belted Colt in a sudden blur of action. But Joshua was even faster. Two guns flamed, the reports merging into one earsplitting crash of thunderous sound.

Borden stayed on his feet for a count of five, swaying as he stared with stupid surprise at the spreading red stain on his holed vest. Gunsmoke hung on the hot still air, spreading into a stratum at chest level and reeking pungently.

Then, as the last echo of the gunfire was replaced by deep silence, the gun dropped with an iron-solid thump from Borden's lifeless fingers. He slumped to his knees, like he was about to say prayers.

'Buck?' Clancey said in disbelief.

Borden gave no answer. He flopped over onto his side with a final, wheezy grunt. Blood trickled from the corner of his mouth and his eyes stayed open but immobile.

Clancey tried to scuttle away down the road like a crab, using one leg and an arm. He started to plead incoherently for his life. But Joshua advanced on him steadily, at which the hardcase panicked and raised and fired his gun all in one swift motion.

Too swift...

Joshua returned the fire with the accuracy to which Clancey in his haste had not given due consideration.

Clancey took the bullet in the head and his death was instantaneous.

Joshua was standing feet slightly apart, long legs braced, smoking Peacemaker loosely held at his side, when he became aware of a smell of burning that had nothing to do with his fired gun. It was coupled with cries and other sounds of frantic activity within the Phillips's house.

He left the sprawled bodies of Sloane's thugs where they'd fallen and started toward the house. By the time he was vaulting the white picket fence, smoke was pouring from the open door and the smashed parlour window. And he could see the flicker of flames inside.

Hornet suddenly shot out of the building, ears flattened, tail between his legs. The dog took off like a rocket, his progress marked by chilling yowls that rapidly receded into the distance.

'Goddamnit! What next?' Joshua asked himself. The cause of the fire was a mystery to him. But he suspected his hard luck was inflicted on innocent parties right down the line this go-round. Joshua? More like he was a *Jonah*.

Each time he went to Felicity's aid, she ended up in a godawful tight. It looked certain, too, that the Phillipses, Mountain Hank and Leigh Jordan were entangled in the latest disaster to befall her.

The smoke inside the parlour was over-powering. Through its thickness, Felicity's streaming eyes could make out only the harsh and terrifying leap of the crackling flames. If she stayed here any longer, she knew she'd suffocate.

She could no longer see how Melville Phillips was coping in his bid to separate Mountain Hank and Leigh Jordan and drag them to safety. But there was the sickly Bess Phillips to worry about, too.

Felicity had last seen her friend passed out in her rocker. If she could just get to the poor woman, revive her maybe, pull or push her chair out the door...

Her plan, barely decided upon, died a-borning. With a loud creak, a whole section of the tightly packed bookshelves, undermined by the fire, swayed out from the wall. The draught of air pushed ahead of the shelves cleared a momentary gap through the smoke as they toppled.

And directly under the shower of dislodged, leather-bound volumes was Bess. Still immobile like a delicate alabaster statue, quite insensitive to the bombardment or the turmoil of the blazing room.

Felicity was horrified. Then the shelves themselves fell across the woman in her rocker with a sickening crash. A dense cloud of smoke, shot with sparks, dropped a veil over the grim tableau.

It was time for Felicity to look to her own survival. Sharing Bess's fate while still conscious was too hideous to contemplate. Gasping for breath, feeling sick to her stomach, she dropped to the floor, where the air was clearer, and crawled on her hands and knees under the worst of the smoke in the direction of the door and, she hoped, eventual safety.

Just before she reached what she thought was the threshold, she was met by Joshua Dillard. Leastways, she thought it was him but there was something wrong about his face. She could only make out a pair of eyes, glaring with anxiety.

She was dizzy from the heat and lack of air. On the verge of blackout, she made an effort to come to her senses.

'The others ... still in there,' she murmured.

But Joshua stooped and hoisted her over his shoulder in a fireman's lift. After that, everything became even more topsy-turvy. Her whole, blurred world, turned upside down figuratively, was now inverted in reality.

He took her out to the road in a jolting run, her arms hanging loosely down his back. There, he knelt and lowered her to the ground, so she was in a sitting position. He put an arm behind her shoulders, and gently lowered her flat to the ground on her back.

She took in great rasping breaths of fresh air and started to regain normal awareness of her surroundings. She saw what it was that had puzzled her about Joshua's face. It was wrapped around with a wet kitchen towel.

But almost immediately, he was up and gone. She struggled to lift her upper body onto her supporting elbows.

Joshua was plunging back into the burning house in reckless disregard of the danger. The front porch and the parlour part of the building looked near collapse.

It was a pulse-quickening spell before he reemerged from the lurid, smoky glare, coughing and spluttering and dragging out Melville Phillips. The doc was struggling feebly, making ineffectual protests.

'It's useless, man,' Joshua said. 'There's nothing you can do for anyone in there. They're lost, I tell you. Go back in there and you'll die, too.'

He looked back over his shoulder. Smoke billowed out of the house, aglow with the backlight of the dancing, roaring flames inside.

The pair came over to where Felicity was and Doc Phillips, whose clothes were scorched and hair singed, slumped down on the roadside weeds beside her. He put his head in his hands. Felicity noticed they were blistered with angry burns, but he seemed to feel no physical hurt.

He looked utterly stunned.

'Melville,' she said tentatively. 'I'm so sorry. What's happened is horrible.'

'What *did* happen in there?' Joshua asked.

Felicity searched her mind, trying to find the logic in something she couldn't begin to comprehend.

'There was the gunfire outside and everybody was confused and frightened. They were asking me questions, wondering what was happening, especially when the front window was smashed... Oh, we should never have come here!'

'But how was the house set afire?'

'It was Mrs Jordan. She pulled out a little pistol and pointed it at me. Hank tried to get it off her, but I think it was Hornet who got her to drop it. Before she did, it went off, breaking a lamp and spilling its oil onto the floor and the fire. There was a tremendous flare-up and everything seemed to be swallowed by flames. So quickly...

'But, Mr Dillard, Mrs Jordan had been pointing her gun at *me*. I think she wanted to kill me.'

Felicity paused, struck by the seeming nonsense of a rich New Yorker trying to murder a no-account, harmless, worthless Colorado farm girl.

'Why should that lady have wanted me dead?'

'Why indeed,' Joshua said, his brows drawn together in a frown.

14

CARVER ELLIOT'S TRUE COLOURS

The fire in the Phillips's house burned itself out, leaving a blackened shell. When the full fury of the flames abated, Joshua went in with buckets of water. Lastly, he used a broad-bladed shovel from an outhouse to destroy the hot spots in the smouldering embers.

He left Felicity Elliot and Melville Phillips in the undamaged barn to comfort each other in their time of loss. He had known such grief himself and, being a comparative stranger to them, he also knew he was not the most appropriate company for either.

Too, he wanted the freedom to think long and hard – which he could only do alone.

He couldn't entertain taking blame for the unfortunate deaths of Mountain Hank and Bess, no matter what other guilt twitched his conscience. From Felicity's account, Leigh Jordan had been the catalyst for those deaths and her own – though one of her unintended victims had been a sick, possibly dying woman and the other a man out of his time, languishing with an infected wound that might have proved fatal to his way of life, if not life itself.

Step by step, he started to piece things together, to assemble a rough-and-ready explanation for the events that had culminated so tragically. He thought that if Leigh Jordan had survived the fire, he might have been able to complete the picture. But without her testimony, forced or volunteered, the filling-in of significant holes was frustrated.

While he did his thinking, and reached conclusions that startled even himself, Joshua took the shovel and dug a grave under the trees at the furthest edge of the paddock.

Walt Sloane's buggy came hurtling up when Joshua was about to lug the corpses of Buck Borden and Chaz Clancey off the roadway and to the newly dug grave. Tied behind the buggy was an old mule from the Elliot place, and on the seat beside the lawyer sat Carver Elliot himself.

'Dillard! What goes on here? What heathen thing have you done with my daughter?' The smallholder was beside himself with pent-up fury, rising to his feet, his voice trembling.

Sloane applied the buggy brake and stowed a whip in its bracket.

'Looks like murder and arson has gone on here, Carver,' he said drily. 'Dillard, come on over here and explain yourself!'

'I ain't your servant, Sloane.' Joshua stood his ground by the two bodies but carried on talking. 'These men were scum of your'n, sent by you to murder me, in point of fact. The arson was the doing of your business partner, Mrs Leigh Jordan no less. And I wouldn't put it past you to be knowing more about that than anyone else hereabouts. I reckon you've got irons of your own in this particular fire, though it ain't panning out exactly as you was planning on.'

Sloane and Elliot clambered down from the buggy, bristling with hostility.

'You can talk a blue streak, Dillard, but it ain't going to save your ass. It's too late for you to hide these bodies. We've seen them, and you're going to swing!'

'Like hell I am.'

'There'll be charges laid. I'll see to that.'

'Trumped-up charges! I'll tell it like it was. They chased me all across the canyon country. They threw lead at me. I beat 'em fair and square in a shootout right here on the road. That ain't no hanging matter.'

Sloane smiled crookedly. 'Says you! Seems to me motive and the evidence will show otherwise. I got witnesses aplenty to say you went up against Borden and Clancey in a saloon in Fort Harper, smashing them up with your fists when they were only funning. Next day, you interfered when they were trying to court Miss Elliot.'

'Court! That's rich. Next thing you'll be telling me this damned old reprobate here is her loving pa and not her vilest persecutor.'

Elliot, who'd been fuming with frustration, shouldered Sloane aside and stood in front of Joshua, spitting his words into his face.

'That's a lie, Dillard! What ordure has the sinful girl been telling you? And in the good God's name, what have you done with her?'

'You're forgetting, Carver Elliot,' Joshua said, keeping his tone as even and dispassionate as he could manage. 'I've heard things with my own ears that would make any moral man's blood boil. From now on in, you'll be messing with me, not her. Understood?'

'She has to be corrected for her own good,' Elliot snapped. 'You overstep yourself with your insulting interference in a man's dealings with his kin. In the name of God, I demand to know where she is this instant!'

'That's the second time you've invoked deity. Well, it won't wash anymore, I'm not telling you. There'll be an end to your tyranny and abuse – leastways, as far as Felicity's concerned. She's a fine girl, and this time she's out of your clutches for good.'

Shaking with all-consuming rage, Elliot, the self-proclaimed man of peace and pure-living, cuffed Joshua in the shoulder with a large, bony fist.

'My daughter – give us my daughter! We have to have her, I say!'

At first, Joshua couldn't believe Elliot had actually struck him. He took two backward steps, to recover his balance and decide what he would do.

By hell! He was sick of the palaver, of hearing Elliot play the hypocrite, and he relished the chance to give the disgusting prig his comeuppance. Now he had it. He tasted blood.

He charged in, head low, swinging his fists into Elliot's midriff, two fast, solid blows.

Elliot backed off, but only to swing a long, booted leg into Joshua's face, not with much impact but enough to smash the lips against the teeth.

Joshua, tasting blood for real, bore in again, feinting with his left, then ducking when Elliot retaliated with a wild swing of his own.

As Elliot reeled from unchecked momentum, Joshua brought his head up right under his large nose. The man moaned, wrapping his arms around Joshua. His nose spurted blood into Joshua's hair.

'I'll kill you for this, Dillard,' he mumbled through the trickling blood. 'I swear I'll break every bone in your filthy body!'

'You and who else, huh?'

But before the fight could be resumed in

earnest, its object called a halt.

Followed by the bereaved doctor, Felicity rushed out from the barn. She'd been alarmed by the arrival of Sloane's buggy and the racket of the shouting match and the subsequent scuffling.

'Pa! Mr Dillard! Enough! There've been too many deaths already.'

The mild Melville Phillips bravely rushed to separate the two antagonists.

'Move apart, I say, gentlemen. Your rough fisticuffs are no comfort or help to Miss Felicity.'

Then Walt Sloane made his play. He joined the fray, hauling out a Colt revolver that had been hidden by the tail of his frockcoat. In one smooth motion, he took the barrel in his hand and banged the butt across the back of Phillips's skull.

Phillips dropped with a single breathy groan.

Joshua was dumbfounded. He turned on Sloane. 'Why the hell did you do that? He's no part of this business.'

Sloane sniggered. 'You don't know the half of what's at stake here, Dillard. You're all muscle, big talk and a fast gun. Well, this time the gun's drawn right now and it's pointing at you.'

He spun the gun in his hand and aimed it at Joshua at close quarters. If it was to come to shooting, Joshua was certain to be the first to catch a bullet.

Unexpectedly, Carver Elliot had ideas of his own. Choosing the moment to reveal his true colours, he snatched the gun from his accessory's grasp and seized Felicity by her hair, bunching it up cruelly and dragging her to him.

Felicity cried out in pain and distress. 'Oh, you beast! Let me go!'

'What say we kill the pair right off – busybody Phillips and the meddling gunhawk both?' Elliot asked.

'Now .hold on, Carver, let's think about this...' Sloane prevaricated.

'I have. We shoot the pair of 'em dead. After that, we get our pretty mistress here to sign the papers making me, Carver Elliot, her sole beneficiary. Then we can kill her, too, of course, and throw all three into the ruins of the Phillips' house. We'll fire it up again and burn the bodies. No one will know they didn't die accidentally.'

'Why, that's brilliant, Carver,' Sloane said.

Felicity struggled desperately, but impotently, to free herself. 'You swine! How can a man treat his daughter so?'

Joshua, who'd guessed at things the girl didn't as much as suspect, took in the changed, more frightening situation, but he still sounded calm, even scornful.

'God almighty, Elliot,' he said. 'You're unbelievable. Where's your high-minded religious claptrap now?'

Sloane laughed. 'He surprises me, too, I'll allow you that. But I think he's between a rock and a hard place if he's to capitalize on what I've told him. Guess his brand of prayer-saying goes out the window till he has secured his fortune. And paid me my share, of course.'

'Glad you find it amusing, Sloane,' Joshua said, gritting his teeth at the enormity of what the lawyer was prepared to condone. 'Maybe you should spare the time to explain what you're hinting at some more. Just so we know how clever you are before our lives are ended.'

Suddenly, he'd seen something that made it imperative he should keep talking, and keep the two blackguards' eyes focused only on what was in front of them. Joshua tried not to let his eyes stray too obviously beyond them and give the game away as he took in the detail.

Lurking behind some stunted bushes at

the fringe of the clump of cottonwoods and aspens was the slimmest of chances that the tables would be turned yet.

15

SETTLING OF ACCOUNTS

Joshua sweated all over. A broiling, summer-afternoon sun beat down on them as he tried to keep surreptitious watch on the bushes. He hoped it hadn't been just his eyes playing tricks on him.

Could it have been the heat that shimmered over the road, creating a mirage that made bushes move when they didn't?

He said thickly through his split, swelling lips, 'Unless I miss my guess, Sloane, it was the picture that put you on the track, wasn't it?'

The lawyer started but affected not to understand. 'The picture? The track? You speak in riddles, man. What picture? What track?'

Good, thought Joshua. He'd grabbed the man's complete attention right off.

'The picture was a tintype that spilled from Leigh Jordan's satchel when she first came here to the Phillipses, trying to buy their property. A photograph of a man and a little child.'

'I don't know what you're talking about,' Sloane said brusquely.

'I reckon you do, Sloane. The man in the picture had features and an inimitable smile that put you in mind of someone you knew.'

'Is that so?'

'Yeah ... Felicity Elliot, who maybe understandably is totally unlike her stepma, *but who also bears no resemblance to Carver Elliot, her supposed father!*'

Carver Elliot growled in renewed fury; Felicity gasped, but not from the fresh pull on her hair; Walt Sloane essayed a smarmy smirk.

And out among the bushes, something was stirring again... Joshua's hopes rose a notch.

'Very clever for a failed Pinkerton range dick,' Sloane said. 'But you'll be dead before it does you any good.'

'Well, it didn't do Leigh Jordan any good when she spotted the likeness, I'll grant you that. When she met the girl in Fort Harper, recognized who she was, and saw she'd immediately enlisted my sympathy, Leigh dumped me like a hot brick.'

'Aw ... a discriminating woman of taste could have any number of reasons for doing that. You're a loser, Dillard.'

'I figure she understood I'd be an obstacle rather than a help in carrying out her real purpose for coming to this part of Colorado – which was to murder Felicity *Jordan*.'

Sloane laughed a dry kind of laugh that had no humour in it. 'You don't say? Sure she didn't take you on to eliminate the kid for her? After all, you're a hired gun, ain't you? Isn't killing what folks pay you for?'

He was needling him, Joshua knew. Playing with him like a cat plays with a mouse before the death blow is struck. But Joshua didn't care. He had his attention. That was all that mattered...

Till what he thought it was in the bushes made its move.

'You've got it wrong, Sloane,' Joshua ploughed on. 'I accept only the jobs that take my fancy. I do what's in the interests of justice and fair play – no more, no less. Leigh Jordan was anxious to have dirty work done, and she was smart enough to figure I was in no wise her man after all.'

The rustle in the bushes was like a

stalking. An advance, a pause…

Luckily, Sloane was too much taken with taunting Joshua, whom he thought was a dead man walking, to notice.

Carver Elliot's attention was likewise engaged by the exchange. But his attitude to it was quite different to the smooth lawyer's.

With a vicious snarl, he barked, 'We've heard enough of this rigmarole, Sloane. Why bait him? What does it matter if he knows too much? He's going to die. They all must die – Melville Phillips and the girl, too, when she's signed the paper.'

'Tut!' Joshua said. 'I think my Bible says something along the lines of thou shalt not kill, Elliot.'

The barb was too much for the self-styled Sin Destroyer. 'You're a fiend, Dillard. Get you gone!'

At that, Elliot flung Felicity aside to the ground and raised Sloane's gun, pointing it directly at Joshua's head.

Joshua knew he could never draw and fire his Peacemaker faster than Elliot could pull the trigger. This time his number was up. He was going to be the loser for good and all, and of something far bigger than just the money – his life.

Almost as though deliberately, Hornet left

his rush from the bushes and his spring to the very last moment.

Mountain Hank's faithful hound Hornet was a one-man beast, at home only in the wilderness at the side of his master. The past days at the Phillips's house had not suited him. Nor had he been happy to see his vigorous man-partner laid low. He had liked the fire that was constantly in the grate, but the soft living had soon palled. He yearned for the freedom of the untamed open spaces of his mountain home.

The very worst that could befall him had followed – the loss of his beloved master in a terrifying fire that was beyond his understanding. The dog was devastated.

Hornet's ancestry was uncertain. In Fort Harper, folks said his mother was a she-wolf, his father an Alsatian, the property of a pioneer family who'd long since quit the country. The she-wolf had come a-courting the settlers' dog, but had later returned, or been chased off, to the wild.

The story went that Hank Montgomery had found Hornet as a pup beside the body of his mother, who'd been caught in a trap in the snows. The winter had been hard and cold, and food very short. Rather than abandon the pup to the mercy of the elements, Hank had tucked the spirited small creature in his pocket, suffering a nip from needle-sharp fangs for his pains, and taken him to his den-like home.

Over the subsequent months, Hank had set to training the orphan. The young dog exhibited an almost human-like cleverness. An expression of trust and love had replaced the fierceness, and the wolf-dog grew into adulthood with his father's Alsatian build plus his mother's wolf-like agility and wondrous keen brain.

But apart from Mountain Hank and a select few that Hornet knew to have his master's approval, all other humans remained suspect.

And Hank's enemies, who included the censorious Carver Elliot, were Hornet's enemies, too. Without question. In fact, such was the dog's loyalty that were it not for Hank's orders to desist, he would have readily attacked any such person who came into his sight and caused offence.

Thus when he returned to the Phillips's property – whimpering as he stepped along on scorched paws and knowing instinctively that Hank had been taken from him forever – Hornet was loaded for bear the moment he scented Carver Elliot.

Then the skulking dog, miserable yet still defiant, saw Elliot fling Felicity, a friend of his master, to the ground and heard her cry of pain.

Disregarding all his hurts, Hornet trotted out from the bushes silently and at the double. Eyes gleaming wickedly, he gathered himself up and launched himself with the speed of light at Carver Elliot's throat.

Joshua flung himself to the right as far as he could leap. The shot that left the Colt in Elliot's fist was wild and wide, but there'd been no knowing which direction the lead would fly.

Joshua was lucky.

Elliot was not. Hornet's savage fangs sunk deep into the back of his neck, tearing a bloody gash and possibly severing the spinal column instantly. Hornet was a big dog, with huge jaws and a powerful bite.

The man fell to the ground without uttering a sound. Hornet threw back his head and gave a deep throaty bark unlike that of any normal domestic dog. He then seized the man by the throat again and shook him like a big, floppy rag doll.

Finally satisfied his victim and old enemy

of many a year was dead, he whirled and fled the scene, back the way he had came, through the cottonwoods and the aspens. Back, maybe, all the way to the wild country.

Meanwhile, Walt Sloane made a dive for his fallen Colt.

Felicity, though bruised, had her wits about her even if she couldn't understand much of what had been said or what had happened. She was closest to Sloane and reached him first.

Oblivious of the throbbing pain in her head where Elliot had held her by her hair, she stamped on Sloane's wrist, and held her foot there with her full weight till he was forced to release the gun.

Joshua glided up and cleared his throat. He was standing over Sloane with his Peacemaker drawn.

'He's covered, Felicity. Are you getting up peaceable, Sloane? Or do I shoot you in the guts?'

Sloane nodded his head. 'You've gotten me in no position to argue, Dillard.'

Felicity stepped back and Sloane rose, his hands lifted in abject surrender. He shuddered when he saw the torn and bloody mess the dog had made of his co-conspirator's throat.

Joshua said, 'It's time we had a long chat, Sloane. You've got a heap of explaining to do before you're off the hook.'

It fell to Felicity to care for the half-conscious, grief-stricken Melville Phillips. Joshua wheeled out another buckboard from the barn, and the Elliot mare Sally was rounded up and put in the traces.

When all was made ready, Felicity gave Joshua a tense, baffled smile, about to set off to take the hurt and homeless doctor back to the Elliot place, where she also had the unenviable task of telling her stepmother that Carver Elliot was dead.

'There's so much that doesn't make sense,' she said. 'All the deception and killing...'

Joshua said, 'I'll have the answers to your questions when I see you next. That I promise. And, if you haven't figured it so already, I can tell you the worst of your troubles is over – for good and all.'

That was true, Felicity knew. Never again would she suffer the unwelcome, seemingly unnatural attentions of Carver Elliot.

Sloane was put up on the seat of his buggy, wrists tightly tied with a leather strap, and Joshua took him back to his office over the dry-goods store in Fort Harper.

The prisoner was nothing loath to get himself quickly out of sight, off the sunlit street. Upstairs, Joshua slung his dusty black hat onto the hickory stand and Sloane into the tub-shaped, cushioned chair behind his desk.

'Now, you cheap chiseller, start talking!'

The crooked lawyer whimpered confirmation of Joshua's guesses about Leigh Jordan. He confessed everything he knew, showing him the telegraph messages from his brother in the New York law office.

Leigh Jordan, it appeared, had had a secret agenda, bigger fish to fry.

'Buying up land in the park for piddling sums, using dummy frontmen, was just a cover-up,' Sloane told. 'From information I procured, I figured out the land-grab she was interested in was on a different scale, in a different place.'

'Do tell. I knew Mrs Leigh Jordan in a sense that didn't include her history or ambitions.'

'Her true mission here was to find her dead husband, Humphrey Jordan's long-lost daughter by an earlier relationship and eliminate her.

'Old Man Jordan – Humph – didn't die intestate, as is widely supposed. Rumour among the legal fraternity in New York has it that Humph willed property on Manhattan Island – the core of his wealth acquired in late life – to a daughter he'd dumped in earlier times of waste and sin after they'd been deserted by the child's ma.'

Joshua nodded as he listened. 'I take it we're talking here about Felicity, who was the child, and her real mother.' He frowned. 'Who was her ma?'

Walt Sloane, pale of face, licked his lips. 'I don't know her name. The old goat Humph covered his tracks as a profligate well. But she was an – uh – unfortunate.'

'A prostitute, you mean?'

'Sure. I reckon she must've been a whore all right. They roamed the West from mining camp to cow town, and she supported Humph on her earnings. He never did a lick of work hisself, they say.'

'So the mother walked out on Humph, leaving him with her baby girl.'

'Right. And Humph was unable to care for the kid, so he abandoned her with an Illinois farming couple, who were Carver Elliot and his first wife.'

'It's not uncommon, I guess,' Joshua said. 'Those farmers all seem to want kids, even when God knows they have enough of 'em.

And the one-time consumptive Elliot didn't seem to have any that were his own flesh and blood. Maybe he didn't have the power, despite his stinking secret lusts.

'But I interrupt. What else did Humph do after his woman had left him?'

Sloane shrugged. 'Maybe the shock of losing her services and his easy living brought about a change of outlook. Anyhow, I guess the old goat reformed. It appears the results were something else. He went to New York City and made a fortune by speculating in real estate. Do you know New York at all, Dillard?'

'Sort of, but I ain't got a detailed map in my mind. I did my history at school and know Manhattan began as a town built at the tip of the island. It was called New Amsterdam and served as the capital of the colony of New Netherlands during the Dutch domination. But it's not my neck of the woods.'

Sloane was starting to feel a mite more comfortable. Coming clean wasn't so hard after all.

'Then you must know that Manhattan Island is the heart and centre of New York. I'm confident it'll stay so, too. It doesn't take a wise man to know that blocks of property there will be worth tens of millions of dollars in the years to come.

'Humph was a shrewd investor. He consolidated his holdings in Manhattan. He knew that one day New York will be the richest and most important city in the world. No man could go wrong if he were to buy up bits of land or buildings in its heart.'

'I guess not. So when does Leigh Jordan start to figure in this?'

'Leigh Nathanson – as she was then – was something of a gold-digger and had a less-than-perfect past herself. Another woman of easy virtue, I guess. Being younger than Humph and still possessed of her looks, she inveigled the old goat into marrying her.

'She was a match for New York's smartest man of business. She wanted name and money at this juncture in her life, and she guessed Jordan's old bones wouldn't last long – specially if she treated him to a high old time. He still had the appetites, but not the stamina.'

Joshua nodded again. He knew just how coolly ruthless Leigh Jordan could be. She hadn't given a damn for conscience or morals in anything. When she had a want, she had her way.

'But after the old man died, things went wrong. How exactly?'

'Jordan's lawyers were unable to trace the missing girl heir he nominated in a scandalously remorseful will. No doubt encouraged by Leigh, they presumed the daughter dead, knowledge of the will was suppressed and the Jordan estate passed to the claimant, his surviving wife.

'Still worried, Leigh then set about striving to secure her position. She hired detectives who established that the family who'd taken in the Jordan infant in Illinois had gone to Colorado. But they got no further. I believe Elliot had gone by some other name in Illinois and changed his name on his second marriage, which may have been bigamous.

'The detective agency recommended yourself to Leigh Jordan as being a man not likely to balk at – uh – unorthodox requirements ... who'd do anything she asked for money.'

Joshua bristled. 'They – or she – read me wrong, Sloane.'

The interview went on to cover again how Sloane had been put on the track of the truth about Leigh Jordan by the photograph of the man and child spilled from Leigh's satchel. Both subjects had familiar features that instantly put Sloane in mind of Felicity 'Elliot', who was totally unlike her pa as well as her stepma.

Once again, Joshua saw how it all fitted, and why Leigh Jordan had been willing, even anxious, to dump him after she'd seen Felicity – so like her true father in appearance – in Fort Harper.

'Well, you rat, running to Elliot with your double-crossing schemes profited you nothing. But here's one last little something you can have for free from myself.'

Joshua got up suddenly, kicking his chair to the floorboards behind him. Then, face hard, he swung a fist across the desk. The angry, pile-driving punch slammed into Sloane's smooth face, making it a bloody mask. His chair rocked over under him. He was out of it, unconscious, when his ass hit the floor.

No one tried to stop Joshua when he went down to the street and rode away in Sloane's buggy.

Later that week, Joshua visited Felicity Jordan and Doc Phillips at what had been the Elliot place and relayed to them all he had learned.

The new Widow Elliot had already left, returning, she'd said, to her folks in the Reformed Presbyterian Church in Illinois, so they had the place to themselves.

'Hornet's role in the affair was rather *deus ex machina*, don't you think?' said Melville Phillips, M.D., late of London.

'Aw, I don't know about that,' Joshua said.

'He was on the scene at critical points all the way through. Maybe the critter did better than me!'

Felicity wrinkled her nose. 'What was that you said, Melville? *Deus* something...'

'It was Latin, my dear. Never you mind for now. I think you've had enough perverted god stuff thrust into your young life for a wee while. Eventually, we'll have to spend some of your exciting inheritance on new books, to replace those lost in the fire. I'll be able to teach you everything you need to know ... even a little Latin.'

Joshua wondered how the educated English widower and the plucky farm girl might fare together. They were an oddly matched couple. Then he took stock of the mutual lovelight that shone in their eyes, and he thought they'd find a way to work it out just fine.

But that was other people's futures. Joshua was ready to move on, the moneyless loser in the business and the lone rider, as always.

The publishers hope that this book has given you enjoyable reading. Large Print Books are especially designed to be as easy to see and hold as possible. If you wish a complete list of our books please ask at your local library or write directly to:

Dales Large Print Books
Magna House, Long Preston,
Skipton, North Yorkshire.
BD23 4ND

This Large Print Book, for people
who cannot read normal print,
is published under the auspices of

THE ULVERSCROFT FOUNDATION

... we hope you have enjoyed this book.
Please think for a moment about those
who have worse eyesight than you ...
and are unable to even read or enjoy
Large Print without great difficulty.

You can help them by sending a
donation, large or small, to:

The Ulverscroft Foundation,
1, The Green, Bradgate Road,
Anstey, Leicestershire, LE7 7FU,
England.
or request a copy of our brochure for
more details.

The Foundation will use all donations
to assist those people who are visually
impaired and need special attention
with medical research, diagnosis
and treatment.

Thank you very much for your help.